THE MIRACULOUS BIRTH, SECRET LIFE, AND LAMENTABLE DEATH OF MR. CHINN

THE MIRACULOUS BIRTH, SECRET LIFE AND LAMENTABLE DEATH OF MR. CHINN

BY ROGER MOSS

PETER HALBAN
LONDON

FIRST PUBLISHED IN GREAT BRITAIN BY
PETER HALBAN PUBLISHERS LTD
42 South Molton Street
London W1Y 1HB
1989

British Library Cataloguing in Publication Data

Moss, Roger, *1951*–
The miraculous birth, Secret life
and lamentable death of Mr Chinn.
I. Title
823',914[F]

ISBN 1-870015-21-5

Phototypeset by Computape (Pickering) Ltd, North Yorkshire
Printed in Great Britain by
WBC Ltd, Bristol

To Gabriel Josipovici
and
Sacha Rabinovitch

AHEM; OR, BEFORE WORDS

O that there is, ah that there be, a point at which all into oneness meets god knows the desire the yearning for it. One oneness all wholly joined where all melts up or down together in bliss. Art beloving the church drink dance and death and all best things in life are there, or disappointing there. Blessed of all impossible. All to be gathered into one flame, flame into a single sea, all to be together from alpha corners of the word to o-my-god, letters unite. All at a single final vanishing. This hymn hum them home at last. The desire the yearning for it.

How much do you yearn? A thousand a year. A thou, my beloved son?

Mother to baby son to boy child to man father brother lover to sister touch to touch touching. O this is Olivia's world, this touched world, loving love whose love loves lover. Viola's girlhood world, loving love whose love loves brother. Olivia and Viola, palindromes and homophones of merging marriageable love (all pals and homos here together, darling) where circling love loves woman loving girl-boy loving as boy-girl man, or what you will or whisper. Sister loving brother back of it all, games of mixed-up doubles, a wantoner tale, a bedtime pharaoh-tale (tut tut) if you incest. This is the all fine and comic ending, happy unending, da capo. The much desired pretend portending. Bedded bliss. Eye into eye absorbed. Hand by hand held. Breast to breast touching. A perfect round, the dance of love, whirl without end.

This was Mr. Chinn's one wish. His chintzy bliss. His own thin sister's mirror-chum. Her cinematic whimsy-mime. Their christmas-time chimera chime. His choice, his charm, his mesh. His harm, his mess.

Or failing that, lads, shepherd-boys and bushy men.

Or failing that, a wife.

Or failing that, a crab, a crone, a clock, a mill, a second-hand shirt—anything with arms.

O the going through life after wife with a mish-mash of such a desire, such high passions unfooled unfilled, the what a pity of it all. Doomed from the stars (though the fall perhaps was not in his stars, but in his cells), bounded to a bad ending. Turning our comet into an old trajectory (no fun intended), dead ending unhappy, the real funereal fire. Game, set, and dead march.

*   *   *

This is what we have to hear. A tale told with tongue and cheek. A tale forsooth, for soothing troubled souls and treble solos. Not omittedly a Fiddlestick Forsyte's sugared saga forsooth, not a lew-grade jam-packed pot-belly or gargantuan bollock-busting best-speller, forged and forgot at wayland's wayside Word-Hoard Smithy—or at all repeatable beach-shops. Know, knot that at all. But a stale of our own slimes, a tale to hold churchwardens from prayer, and old men from the chippy on the corner. A kind of dumb, thin, queer book, a crap-book of old cuttings and remarks, a slum volume. A must, a piece, in its own little weight.

Great jokes from little achings grow, from little inkhorns. And this is a veriest forest of pinings and ash, a jingle-jungle full of wild games, a grove-yard of broken promise, an unclipped bush thicket (a tuppenny-ha'penny farewell to nowhere), a paranoid maze without a home. You are about to disinter a densely worded tract of tree-felling importance, a whole trunk-full of waste papal, load of bull—an ill-omened hated man you scrapped, his toiled ordure papers, his writ, his rot.

All of it done in dead words threw out, in farced phrases, discarded language needs decoding. A neither here language of the centre, nor there. It's all Chinnese, all croak to me (frogs begin at Crawley). Stale and stolen from Ewell and Morden my words, or from the revered Pinner, carolling this jabbering walkie-talkie. Dead middle, all of this muddle, an art of daftness. Fun and games much less than half a wake, the poor man's choice, a collide-a-spoke. A melting mouth-slaughtering language, cobble-de-cooked up in plots and puns of toneless style. A fracas, say. Discomposition, this scrambled oeuvre, omelette without the pranks.

Now reel on, real one.

MR.
CHINN
WON

A GENERAL
ALLERGY

This is how it was for Mr. Chinn.

Oompah, Oompah, Ocean, Earth; Oops and Polyps; Ammon, World-Egg, and Cheops with everything; Madame Thoth-Ostrich, Osiris and a Dam; from Alf and Betty to Armageddon; Be-All to Heimdall; Great-grandad, Grandad, Ishtar and Yankee-Doodle; Adamandeveandpinchmewell, Ouch, Titter, Titan; begat Typhoo, Nig-Nog and the Cyclops Satanica (for there were gents in the earth in those days); Dr. Seuss and Follow-My-Leader (weighed down upon the swanee's ribcage) begat Castro and Polacks, and Hell-on-Earth and Aspidistra; Mahaleel begat Jared, begat Tom and Jerry, begat Derry and Thom's, begat Harrod's, begat Miss Selfridge, begat Bedadshedid (at the time of Duke Ellington, the flood, and all that jazz); Baghdad begat Bagshot, begat

7

Upshot, begat Upanishad, begat Uberalles; Hair-Loss, Asparagus and Runnymede, begat Tros, begat Trish and Kevin, begat Diomed (who was a girl's best friend); begat Homer Khayyam, begat Diaries and Dictates, begat Gobbledegook, begat Perspex and Farex (who fought together until the land was overcome by Acrilan); Hiawarthur and Guindermere, the Lady of the Lake, begat Galahad, begat Helluvalad; Siegmund and Sick-Linda begat the Walsung Matthilde; begat Nietzsche and Kultur, begat Karl and Groucho, begat James and Joyce, and Flann-Again and Dylan; begat Spiced Mulligatawny, Seagone and Old-Salt Peter (and all Sailors and Yachtmen); begat Venus and Vagina, begat a begum in a big hat and a bigot with a big gut; begat Dad. Who begat Sis and Mr. Chinn, who stuck it out longer than some.

To all of this inheritance he in time retracted. Developed an elegy for it. Came out in a rush.

HIS FURTHERING AND SMOTHERING

Now Mr. Chinn's Dad was quite a caretaker was Mr. Chinn's Dad, but not for himself. Quite a bit of a ladder, a sociable climber, he was, tall and tender, smiley sly brown eyes, sly boots, sleek brown hair slicked with his social greases. Charm the pence off you. A bit of a one for the odd drink the fillies the fellows a flutter and on the side a bit of a one. Not one to be housebound, and beneath a tall a weak kind of a kind man (generous to a fool), soft to the touch, the spoilt of the earth who disapprove with age. To put it finely, it was what he inherited that was the rune the unmasking of him, his own father's weak will. And so it always runs, like legacies and notaries, in the family.

Bought him an early grief. O he with it bought all for them, brought bunches boxes bagsful home from his trivials and

9

traipsings abroad. Shock (ooh la la) delights, and trifles, and other surplus prizes. A houseful of hothouse orchards. Never came home without being loaded, parcels, presents and fuchsias all ripped open in ribbons and beaux for each, and much-laughed stores of tearaway places.

But for himself bought only so much blues and baccarat, too much lacquer and lacking too much sleep. Left him a bad liver and approaching certain debt. For his merry moments, his little kindnesses, his little children when the news was hurt, had that certain mourning after feeling. O Dad Daddy Papa Pop we miss you moan you misused you so, who were always ready with a ruddy smile ready for a laugh large red moustache hardly remember your big ready face at all, your tall sighs beyond our reach, miss you, your highness, for your huge huggings and your homecomings, bags under the arms, the eyes, hung over the banisters to see—your laughing children, always inner thoughts.

But he had been no much for Mummy. She who had mattressed beside him beneath herself, no last love between them. She had been banjo played second fiddle to a sweet soprano in a hotel-suite, sang a little, danced a little, sometimes all ensemble, played a liddle-diddle-di-do to any ass incite. Moved in the better sparkles of sobriety, prim at proms and proper with her programme. Known in the town for all her airs and grace-notes, her pretty hair and bracelets. Had heidi ideas of herself, and idolised her father. He who was big in balls and chain-stores, firm as iron in his ironmonger's firm, a selfishly made man, great sheik, one year the mayor she dotes, and how she dotes. Always there was a framed upstanding photo of him in the full dresser.

She, his only doter, as she never failed to mind them all, could have married a blancmanger with the natural provisional, a mason, a peer's son in the drivelling brush trade, was propositioned by a Highly Street practiser of great dissections. And then all this would not have been. She would have lived in hen-laid on easy-thames instead of in penury on end. Had there not been a passing fashion, an excess of designs upon him, for a stranger in passing. And some looks between them both. There was none too wise about it at the time, they made a handsome-looking double, no debt at all. Coupling on the dancefloor, she liked his manly tang, o she liked his cheek to cheek. She was balled over, wished off her feet, asked for her hand and before she fully knew what she would wear, or where she was, she was his pride to be. Was it his laugh at first sight, sigh at last? Certainly she had liked his smile, his smell, his twinkling ivories.

Within six weeks, and she the weaker sex was given away by her father with grave misgivings. With him six weeks more, and all was ill between them. The hen moans had just begun. Gone from bed to bad to wars, this illusion to dissolution. Theirs to neither was a last longing lover fair. They almost always both instantly regretted it constantly, and grew together an ever-loathing couple. With her pretty there was a stubbornness he had not burgeoned for. With his jolly there was a frivolity, a lack of drive alack, for which she could only fuel contempt upon condemning. She for her father's tough, he for a feather touch soft, ness always yearned. This the gap between them always yawne d.

But within all of this despite, some mean times later she he together teemed and spawned. Their mute comfort sought each other still, furnished a womb between them both, beginning of the jest. Brought them together a little, a little baby gurgle, their fussed child. Now they were not mean and waif alone, but knotted Dad and Mummy, mated and pater of tiny feet, little fingers' ends held them rapt together. Nappy families. Indissoluble, in this horrible, relationship. Till death us two part. Wish it eventually would.

IN WHICH MR. CHINN IS BORED

In those days (it was before and after a war, and in a time of funny peace when an uneasy truth was maintained between us and them) C. & A. send out Ada Cree, that all the world should be tricked. It was for the sake of some cheap pugnacity, fun and fame for all the fumbling, a little midsummer thing for the kiddings. And 'Auntie' Ada Cree was there, the Children's Our Favourite from the worry-less, announcing the praise-winners and seeing that everyone blissfully verged on merriment. There was sinning and glancing in the park that day, a furtive restive atmosphere, near bedlam.

Dad went up to be tricked with Mummy, and Sis too (it was a so kind birthday trait for her). And Mummy won some odour toilette and smiled of it everywhere. Auntie Ada said, 'There's no need to be afraid,' and handed round free boxes of choc-a-blocks to them all, because there was no room for them in the warehouse. But Mummy only ate a bit, and kept the rest for later, guarding it in her frock. Mummy was careful like that.

The Shepherds were there, their next door-knobbers, and Mr. Shepherd's hired spirits got the bottle of him when he suddenly burst out singing to his hotty-toddy daughter, 'Gloria's an ex-Chelsea deb.' O everyone's tempers were sorely frayed when they thought it might have been heard on all the wavebands and aired to multitudes. Gloria Shepherd went into a skulk, and 'So rude,' staid Mummy said behind-hand crossly to Dad, 'an insult to his hosts.'

Also the three Wisemans (Grandpa, Malcolm and Bertha) came up from the west country, wanting to see the show of the star, though Grandpa had a cold coming. It was unquietly quite an occasion, a day for silly prating, sweets and light refreshments all handed round, good booze for all the men.

But what made it a later date remembered, unregrettable, was that in the assortment of it all, Mummy (who was eight mouthfuls all gone) began to feel unqueasily unlike inside herself. Put it down to thirst at first for the sweet milk choccy melting inside her. But then all of a sodden sitting there during their merry piccaninny in the wreck the weather and her waters broke at once. A lightning flash, a flush and loud collapse of Mummy and thunder. O the kiosk, o the fiasco of it all, in all this sticky jammed together corroboree, with everyone running helter-skelter for shelter, unenlightened and sundered, and Mummy in a strange con-traption with sirens ringing rushing headlong eternity-wards.

Whilst outside it rained on and on, catastrophes and doggedness, poured on poor Dad and Sis standing sopping waiting with the so sweet taste still on their lips, hardly knowing what yet had hatched. Parturitions of what was to

13

come in the last annals, this downpour tends to suggest. Portent of a life that was yet to be guttered, of a death not by draining. All a cock-up, this conceiving, from the upset.

And yet Mr. Chinn was born. Too big e'en at the beginning, pre-mature for sure. Came into this world fully-clothed, sporting a twee-jacket with leather patches, and on the breast, all ready to rat about them, three sharpened pencils (because, of course, there was no ink for him in the womb). A natty navy tie not to be forgotten. And a pair of smart brown brogues. This was his early clothing. Middle-aged from the word no, and never the less. Yet never truly grew to manners either. A sort of Petrified Pun in nivea-nivea land always looking for Wednesday.

'O will you look at the little man,' the middle wife crowed, not knowing of whom she spoke—the wan and lonely Mr. Chinn, son of aversion, born to tears. Crooned Chinn of Chinns, a piece of print, a manual, a totally unjustified type, sans seraphim. In the beginning just one word, first entry of the log. Reigned on and off forever, our man. Always waning, ever since.

Such are the manacles of this world, for truly it was a mad ridiculous miraculous begetting to begin with, a mad-summer day's scream, a nine-month's wonder. Bairn of the day that was his sister's both-day two, amidst such all-gender levelling, such free volatility, and with free gifts—All-Gold, French scents, and more. A red saturnalia latterday, putting behind him then all that was to be in storm for later.

Naturally, all this brought Mr. Chinn to be a starry in the press. Not Flea-Street but a porter from the local peepers gave him and Mummy a semi-column and a photo, a splash with the deadline, 'Baby Is Born At Sweet Treat Meeting':

This crowded mum really has something to be poured about! Not only did her booby arrive on his two-year old sibilant's sum-day, but it all happy after she had been

14

gifted a reprise by 'Auntie' Ada Cree at a loon-packed day up in Logjam town. Isn't baby sweet!

The public prince. Clipped this cutting out ever since, the press piece, and shone it round with pride at all available apertures. Got it out religiously regular at all shared birth-dates. And there they were. Mummy holding smiling in her one hand baby, and in her other freehand cheerily the later shock she won. And half a stone, in half-tone, little pint-sized Mr. Chinn only too dazed to hold, himself imprinted in block and quite, an undoubtful fact.

SURLY
LIFE

Fast things they do, fork you out, give you a wide birth, have you in stitches, splice you a knot for your bell-bottom, stop and slap you, make you yell ow, make you breathe deeply briefly bravely of their little sun and air. That's the ploy. Soon as you're suckled, wrenched it off you, get wind of their next. Find you dummy in the corner, snatch that away. Enough to drive you on and off the potty. Keep you removing is their motto presto, harried along there, if you police; behind it all the power of a standing Mummy. No hating aloud, no waiting, no watching. Get you to bawl crawl walk talk read ride quicker than you can, quicker than any rest. Endless prep for endless separations they force you to injure. So they bang you up. Best we forget. Thence to the small murkiness of infinite amnesia.

For his earliest mammaries, Mr. Chinn had none not fed to him in faded photos, or very few. The nice paper-clip, for an instant. That looks like me. Snap. Same ears there, everywhere same squinting eyes, same squashed nose, same squat him. Same famed Chinn. Here, I knows him, only smaller, sitting in the prim, and proffering sighs.

And all of them, all saying that looks like me too. Made in the homage of his Dad, a bit of Mummy here, and for good measure a look-in of his godmother in her eyes too. All features great and small accounted for. All longings to be someone else, himself.

Related all in camera. Photos of aunts and uncles, familiar haunts and unfamiliar angles, great-gran's spangles, cousins' ankles, seasides with Sis and him besides, see-saws with him and Sis bestride, Mummy and Dad and Dad and Mummy, often all in one (Dad would time the shattering with a buzz, and come grinning into the slide of the picture). Family groups, familiar stoops. Aunt Eater and Uncle Belly, Uncle Album (hair all cut off), Uncle Lens (though somehow the son got in), a distanced blurred cousin (once she moved), and Grandma Chinn (with any baby's latest body caressed in the family arms). Some who died, and some who never had children, who couldn't bear each other. Some uniforms, some sunny farms (no one remembered where), some funny frames. All insipid, all in sepia, all separated, stuck in their little corners, and scripted scrupulously in black and white, the volumes of the ancient kodaks, the Book of Ours. Old times in monochrome, kept at home for filmy gatherings, opened with who's and ha's, and then snapped shut for another tome. Until all is a shame and scramble in unassorted boxes, after circa nineteen thrifty-late.

The rest in unrelated figments. Crazy walking on the wobbled paving in somewhere time. Out in his ski-blue leather leading-strings, walking on the top of Mr. Adrian's wall, keeping his brilliance, singing and dancing in his reins.

17

Crusty leaves blown in dusty outhouses at grandma's webby house.

The windy bedroom window growing larger in the dark, and larger still till all is swelled into its sweep.

A car-ride with a perfect strangler after stranding in the blithering snow.

Over and again overhearing shouting in a shut-off room, usually Dad and Mummy on accounts of money on a sad day afternoon, wranglers as clockwork.

Once in a jew jangler's shop in a black-room somewhere, heard violet scheming, colourful language, words of a puce, and stood amongst the tock-tock grimmer of their piles of shiny haemorrhoids and rabies and diabolic rings and clocks and watches, little hand in big hand holding, uneasily watching and waiting with Mummy.

Standing, all moist in fears, too staring scared to dare go on the swing, with Sis and all friends standing round yelling him to have to let it go.

Always this, this dareless standing back, black-looking on in near or fear. This was all that Mr. Chinn mumbled from the beginning: spanned his days there often looking after and onto a fear-filled world, in watching which with his quasi-cool look he will not ever quite belong. 'I am,' he would snap, 'a chimera.'

MEMBRANES OF THINGS PAST

For a long time he used to go to bed early. Well, you generally do at that age, don't you? When only a little morsel, little master Chinn.

Mummy used to watch him thoroughly in the sinking songs together while she dried getting him into his magic plum-jam pies, so that he was ready a bedtime story waiting for the happy bending over him to say: Get nigh, sleet eye, gobble ess, swede reams. All tucked upstairs thoroughly and first asleep by the age of half-past seven, a little-un's teddy on his feet. Sis had an extra half after, being the elder. He would lie, tense and imperfectly sleeping, the younger pretender, hearing their laughter and voices, and at last with sleep the feet-steps up the steep staircase bringing.

This the nightly rite he went through, the bathday

baptism, him and Mummy, total emotion. This the almost nuptial ritual between them bathed, keen cleansing of his flesh of her flesh moulded by the laying on of her hands to his head, blessing and bathing with her cares his hairs, with her caress his arms, the wishful washing and embalming of her descendant's feet, all of it done in a basin. Into her face his gaze facing, with the old gas-geyser gushing and roaring. Sons and loofahs.

Buried him then in shroud-white goodnight tight across him fleece, head resting on billows to carry him over, pushing one foot featherdown into the bed, either down into the fresh clean cold white wetness, pushing him out across the water in his little all alone bed's nest sloop, out into the ship-deep, sheep-dip counting, sleep-clouded, bed-sheet, wing-beat fleet floating dreamworld. He was her charge, her spark, her little beau, her buoy, her boat. Last kiss still glistening his lips, slumbering mumbled his Mummy's double, his trembling there, his tiny troubles, his tummy rumbles, in his dreamy trail and twirl. She awash with wishing watches him the little lamb, her limb, leave his nighttime mooring, gently snoring, knowing the tethers that hold him to her well, keep him and her together. Knowing that the morning tide will bring him back to her for sure without thinking, without ever having been in flight from her, afloat, afar away.

Thus relation-ships are launched, may god bless all who fail.

Next it was Sis and him bath together, thin white twinned legs intertwining in the bubbles, each regarding without shyness she-ness and little he-ness. He was dad and she was mummy, they would marry, with a bubble of their own, keep it in her tummy. Living out in the florist's all on their lonesome, with lemon squash and squirrels, and with no moans or quarrels, barbarians in the wood, so they planned and planted it.

Soap gets in your eyes on bath-nights however tight you are screwed against it. We are thin skins, surrounded in our thinking with kith and kin and singing. Easily things sink in, and easily we sting. Mr. Chinn was not excepted, easily accepted all this thing, soaked up his existence without seeking, self-absorbed, took it all in. He was made this way, knitted up the whole sponge-bag of himself he was kitted out with, the bag of layers we lie upon one another liar to liar laying, filling us up with who we are, how we live, love and have obedience, the body of our knowledge before we even know it, saying, Carry on for me, repeat the burden. So old whining is put into new battles, and so we are each easily contented to be so contained. Readily Mr. Chinn learned to speak the same luggage, to hide in the same skin.

Soap stings eternal. The semi-permanent maimed brain.

HOME
COUNTS

All the houses Mr. Chinn was born to death in all the same all had the same stuck-up all stucco look same short front back and sidegate. All privet, keep out, no let up. Highly expectable, secure and safe as houses, and, all things delivered, very nice. Smile upon unbroken smile of it. He was baby stucco.

All semi all in a row with the other half of their lives lived by the other half wanting to know how the other half lives. Cemetery about a line. Each a lawn unto itself, with housewife Jean smiling to housewife Joyce across the boundary washing-line in spite of wishing what last night at what o'clock in the morning frightful heard through the clarity walls had happened to shake her up. Her audacious boarders.

They had the country in their front stained glass (a minor

morris hearths and crofts touch), and standing in it always with his nose pressed Mr. Chinn could believe himself in a rose-coloured, untainted world, until his own held breath missed it away. Others had sunbursts or sets of birds cawing back to their roots in theirs, simples of homely nest.

A step inside and it was a neat and tiny do-up do-down world, just tight for Dad and Mummy, Sis and Mr. Chinn, a bijou-box, streets out of the identical homes expedition, a place all of their loan, where they could whittle down and spin the reminders of their lives.

Everywhere there were flaws that people stood on, covered over, and all their wellingtons they kept in the cupboard. Mummy shows her choosing in the leafy carpet, the flowery covers on the oozy chairs, the neat nest-egg of tables, the formal florals lining the walls and the normal floor all lino'd in the hall. Her match-all tasting is reflected in the con-formed mirror over the fireplace, in the lamps which are standard, the fixtures hanging on the walls (hassled scenes, crimes of old london, a spatial constable), and in the family trays from which she serves her cosy three-piece tea-set. This is the settled unsubtle look of it for always, the curtained certainty, nothing out of place, nothing left uncovered, everything left to chintz, everything stuck in the dull ticking of the square uneclectic clock with other knicks and un-knocked knacks in the same mental-spaces as the next-door nobodies, and all the hoard of neighbourhood mantles all of an abiding peace. The decoration of dependence.

During their wake-days, life evolved around Mummy. For Sis and Mr. Chinn she was always there, theirs to dress wounds, sew dresses, caress and cuddle, blow out candles, hand out bowls of alphabet-soup, stop and stoop to hear their alphabet, or their tables, lay the table, label their clothes, close their drawers, praise their drawings, say their prayers, make them say please. She it was to home they were bound for maternity, their total local world. She would give them

23

esher twickenham off when they needed it, make them say surrey. Norwood the egham staines on their faces pass unnoticed. She was the one surbiton thing in their woking lives, a source of ealing. Or so it cheamed.

Dad was more on the emergings of their lives, at work or away, and only there for blank holidays or work ends or late out and not at all. It was a rare occasion he would be back too late for suburbs, tipsy-toeing in from the reel-away satiation, and just in time to creep up to them for an extra story and into them for tuck.

There were two stripes tyrewide of concrete on the drive for Dad to sermonise their first car on Sundays, and two steps footdeep of paving to the lawn for Mummy kneeling to snip and worship the household larkspurs and petunias. Kept themselves each a separate part after the weak endless usual unfinishing financial contumely. Voices in hidden chiding, Waste all gone then, Dues I want with moan. Once or twist burst out with hell and dead and leave and go then. Then Sis and Mr. Chinn sat palely with the playthings saying nothing, not even looking, with the dread mournful weighting of heaviness hanging not understood above them. Teatime passed stiffly polite, blighted, hardly a chink, and the evening stifled on the sofa with the papers, the Tell-it-gruff or on Sundays the Excess, always an unfinished cross-word between them. Morning day came lighter with re-life, Dad whistling off early for his train, and Mummy bisselling around to punish everything in sight with dusters and with vigour.

ENGLISH
LESSENS

And then the widening rule-book with its ritual. The shy thin mournful faces, cringing like slaves. Went willy-nilly to school. This was the sickened age of Mr. Chinn.

Whistles and bells sounded for hours and ends. Made him do as he was tolled. He was schooled and scolded, ruled over and underlined. Dad and Mummy said, 'He needs to be stretched,' and certainly he was taught.

They taught him riddling and writhing (churned-up writhing with a fainting pain), spoiling and minding his bees and queues, the rude amounts of hysteria (tense tickly sex, and all that), joggers and infinity. He learned his two tide-tables off by yacht, what tutus are for, and why free chews are sick. He was addled, distracted, mortified and derided all at once.

25

They were the first to introduce him to improper fictions and the nearest dismal places. This was the startling-point for his much-ado, his adder-lessons.

And all the time they also teased him how to stand or sit or walk in a silent straight line (the sharpest difference between two pains), fearing the head and disposing of the body. To sit and walk in pairings (chairing his desk with Hugh Juggly, the fat unfit overfed unlively boy who picked himself and Mr. Chinn at every importunity). To sport the team (though he always got away from the fit bawling machos when he could). And every morning, when the school dissembled, to feel to the full its false falsetto unison, singing with disgust, 'O, we shall build Jarrow slums in England's grim and pleasant land.'

He remembered them all, wondering what became of him and him and her, the other members of his kingdom, class and order, from Alfred Abbott, Brian Box (the batter of Britain, the bowler-hit), Mr. Chinn imps-elf, and May Donne-Hood (the English rouser, the little Miss Peach), all the way to Ada Zed. Amongst them all his best first mate with whom he played out daily games of knights and dragoons and sea-going ex-piracy, with fire-away vie-urges and cries of, 'I shot thee, Albert Ross!'

And this is what they were and who they were to be: Form 2B, regimented, registered and ledged, ticked off by name to be a class, learning by rote the rite of the right lines set them. So that the master, the monster, who took them for all the subjects and the abjects of their languishing, Mr. Able, terrible with his cane and all his abilities, he will teach them, 2B, what it is to be in England English. O, 2B in English know that Able's there. And when that Mr. Able in his sharpest suit has punished the dregs with a route-march (for uphill is the cruellest march), and bothered every boy with his switch and a licking, of which aversion engendered is the fear—then what? Then you can be sure that every last letter tiptoeing on

26

the English tongue, from Able to Braining to Courser, will be tinged with this touch of a lashing, a lasting stinging, and the stigma will be carried on in every accent, act and utterance of this, the bullying doggerel breed.

So that Mr. Chinn who always before had his head in a book on his lap, a real lap-reader, a true book-murmurer (it was his only way of shutting Mummy up and out) became now, like all of them, an ill-letter-hater, a mutter's boy, a lost utterer, for whom sullenness was beholden. The saturnine tales had caught his tongue. This was the meanness by which they were all drained.

THE MIRROR'S TALE

After every suchlike satchelled prolonged daytime came the night, flying our kite with a palamino (the ones with the longest tails) in a far-off paired-off flee-away land, coupled brothers in each other's arms, and no homily or thesis to spoil the fun. Dream-boating in a land of nudes and noddy as he grew, dreams of the rude, fun to see. His sleep as yet was an uninterpreted uninterrupted unnumbered slumbering, an unsombre thing.

After every night the awful daily jawful of the mirror begins. Washing or brushing his dreadful headful or mouthful, or shaving his youthful cheeky lippy cheerful chin, or standing regretful entirely renewed, full-length in undressed reversals, reflexing his missing muscles, holding his shudders back, and his puniness up a little while he looks, the fearful truthful figure in the glass stares gazing on. Always the same terrier-stricken dog-eared edgy face, dirty paws, damn nose, cross eyes.

Verity, verity, all is fantasy, all is revelatory. This dour wry me, this unideal platonic so-far-so-good image in one-to-one scale, this see imager, this be-flattered mine—this was the him he had to live with, his accompaniment. Trying with handled admirers within admirers, for hairs on end, to see the blackhead of his forehead, his fair hair and all as it was seen. Trying this brag-to-front way to know himself as a better, and ending knowing only at best a neither, a twice-affected double of himself in half-piffle, him prismed, aghast. But never ending this unbroken cycle, this mad oval cracked mirror game of self rear-guard and re-recurred self-loving and self-loathing, seeing both himself as a deity little horror and a dirty great hero.

Looking back upon himself all this time, who did he think he was? He had versions of himself as a great lover, a great leader, bringing crowds to their fate with his elegance, his harlotry, at sweltering rallies, church-halls and little hecklers. As a grey doctor on the broads, a lean ham, a charmer, the derivative amulet of his generation, to the implausibility of hordeless countenances. An entertainer, an undertaker, the asthmatic leader of a small malicious, a surgeon-major, performing undercover operations in the dark. A variety chameleon, cheering them in the gaiety, the happy, the play-dome, or a straight musician, a basker in the shade, an organ-grinder manqué working the rodgers and hammersmith music-halls. A virtuous lightning-fast conductor with his finger on the baton, and the leading cart-horses of the world under his reign. It was clear only on reflection that he was going to be a maestro, a maelstrom, a mistral, a world-winner. He would be the adoring young man on the flynn trapeze, the armstrong hero, the best-selling novello, the kin-needy fonda of a famous die-nasty,

the man who broke the fairbanks at molto bravo, astaire, a
star. From early on, Mr. Chinn was privately perfectly sirius,
the dogged stare, the little dreamer-boy.

BIG
CISSY

I n all this guileless golden age, at any time from ten to four,
home in any form with shorts shirt and cap and tie
(Mummy with her smart skirt and cup of tea), Mr. Chinn
was out-worldly matched the same, wee kin weak out. His
angular sexton looks, small fissures, peeled skin, thin skinny
bland and blue-eyed boy, bored grin, high piping harping
hoping non-stop sexless ceaseless voice.

Sis, on Mummy's other hand, was dark, unfairly beautifully maid, dutiful, demurring, preserved and solemn silent.
Was this a start of all that Mr. Chinn was not and wished
himself to be? It was such dark pouting poise he later sought,
such dim unshouting churls and boys, the sort of fine-limned
well-made self-possessed proportion he was drawn to. This
and the gloss-eyed fate-crafts he first saw in the black-sheep

barbers' shop, looking through the nudes-papers at all the birds and breasts and bushes. Or at the furtive mag-shots in the back-street nosey-urgent, the cockles and muscles all-lithe all-lithe o. Was this and Sis, so neat of next of skin, the source of such desire to be himself in another, seeing in her in them the sylph-like brothers, the self-sired lovers? Was she the double of all his troubles, the one he could not win?

She was his protector and protester through and through this time. When he was in trouble and tears, in cold or wet or tired or in prostration, she was his soother, smoother, saviour, mother. She saw him right through, drying his eyes or his hair, or crying too or he with her in simultaneous pathetic sympathy. When he was a know-all coward, holding back or forth in front of circles or cycles of friends, or anywhere, because he was always voluble and feeble together, she was his greatest laugher, his gravest loather. And when he was a freud (and he was a bag of new erotic simperings almost from the time of his bath) he turned his tale and ran to her. As when the club-footed bungle-owner chased him from his back with torn shorts and pantings. Or one long snowy whimper, when he would not get on the slay-edge, fearing his death of cold. Then only she could be his elder and abettor, his backer, his side-kick and ally, Sis.

When he or she was at their wet's end day, they would play for each other. They would take turns on the piano loudly, pretending to be conceit-monsters on the nostrum, thrashing out their skirls, their misericords, their half-perjuries (Mrs. Watser came on ivory tunes-day for their lessons, and always lost her tempi). They would sing together in puny song their cursory dreams: the singer in her council-house, chanting out harmony, the old man who couldn't pay his rates, and Friar Jack and Sirrah Jane who lived up the hill and down the lane. Or they would get out the messing-up box, all the unwanted rugs and hatters and sporting for each other's amazement, and always waiting for the bottom of the box where the fox-stole lurked with staring eyes, like an ominous nameless thing, and where with a special frill they came to Mummy's discorded bridewell-gown and Dad's paternal slithered dancing shoes. It was playing with each other in every way that they began to learn the old Chinn-Sis game of snakes and ladies, the A-dame and Evil game that Mr. Chinn never quite got rid of the hunger of, never got nearer the nectar, the knack.

All together on certain days they would go hand in hand and hands in pockets down to the shopping to spend their pence. Parade along the rows of names of Geo. Fredk. Wm. Chas. & Sons La Mode Kandy Korner and Ltd. Goods for everything all remembered with perhaps a list ticked off for Mummy, her errant children. They would stand reflecting in the window of the little sweat-shop on the corner (lickerish all-slurps, slobbered sucks and gobbled sticks) or the troy-shop by the blank (wooden horses, dolls in priams, building blocks for toppling towers, plaster of paris soldiers). After a whole while glazing they would make their pent-up choose, their lolly-buy, push the door pinging open, and step to the counter to speak their please. Once at only eight and six they went off after school, pretending for a walk, to the nurse-man's green house to buy a bunch of sweeties or forget-whats for mother's day—coming home to you shouldn't have, with all that terrific, o you are two kindlings. So step by step they learned to buy, to bide their time, to save and savour for all they bought. To buy, to shop, purchase to dream. Choosing between goods and maman in all the rest of the rust of their add-up ma'am and sir-fêted lives. Small change.

OUTSIZE
WORLD

D ad and Mummy came to this carnage of a world with all the other outwardly mobile masses. It grew ahead of Mr. Chinn, walling in the free spaces, cloistering in on him. It was a new fouled land, a nowhere superber, the sudden region, where all before them had farmed old plough-land. This that they call Meadow Lane was all daisies and a bull before the bulldozers came, and Strawberry Close was fields ripe for the picking by around mid-June, and that dead square of corpse, railed round in rusting green, was then real living woodland joined up to what is now the links, now that envelopment's got their hands on it, no expanses spared. All pastoral history now.

The bits he grew to know best bit by bit were the over-grown remainders of this past, the undergrowth, the untouched mucked bits left aside for refuge. Behind the hindermost compost-heaped backside of the back-garden, the grass-cuttings and the rustic guttering on the tottering raked reeking cob-wobbling shed, there was a gaping in the fence for the escape and escapades of boys, just three slats wide. Off into the dank brambled ankle-scraping underworld of scraps and nails, sharp pains and nettles, wet docks, and smashed stag bottles. There he and Albert and the tribe would squeeze the thick sap happily from stalks, stalk and talk in wisps among the long grasses among themselves. There they would squat squashing woodlice, telling white lies, would lose themselves for hours in the thicket of hunting ants or in the battle and burial—with full millipede honours—of bugbears and beetles. This rubbished unravished waist-high wasteland was only theirs, a world of leavings and behind. Mr. Chinn began to know himself a part in all this damp and cramp. Here he learned to his fingertips the language of death and dump.

Friends and alleys all met up for play, ringing bells to get them, to get him, together. Gathered for tag along the pavement, counts of ten and shouts of bags and when you can be got, and when you can be god, and jingles of niggers for beginners by the toe, and games of chants, of can't catch me, and cries of glee, for a toffee-flea. All their playing sayings, all the meanings of their miny-mo.

Up to the woods for copse and rabbits, hideaways and secrets. And into the hedges of the prairie gardens for choirboys and andeans, coming home with a grassy pair of knees. Blood-tingling brotherhoods, solemn packets, smoke-signals, and swearing, Can you keep a cigarette?—with the played out matches falling to the ground. A time of secretions, of uncertain knowledge, fibs and fabulous tale-telling, everything possible in haven and oath.

This from tea to bedtime, or for whole days on the run, taking in more and more, the new world of the fields beyond

35

the marooned munificent housing-scheme, wilder still and wilder. The allies' adventures in wander-land, and through the working-classes and what the allies found there. Already on the edges of Mr. Chinn's protracted world there were stranger folks from whom he kept his disdain, dustmen-demons you would cross yourself over to avert, aged neutered ogres shuffling and snuffling by, whiskered and small and smelling of whisky, and staring smeary children of incomprehensible uncalled-for sprite and spiking, prickly sickly little elves. Once it seemed a bad fury had granted him three witches throughout his life: an old woman who called foul gnomes to him from the bus-stop, a fat lady in the chops who tried to pinch his cheeks or his change, and a big girl who stalked after him blowing babbles, and wanted to be cursed or kissed or see his wee.

But past these outlandish monster hostilities, escaped from their glowering ardours, there were the uplands, the downlands and the foothills, where they could footle and begin to feel what it might be to be themselves, alone and free, or tell themselves that fable. Once upon a half-term, in these same hols, they came on a woodman bending in the grass, who took them up and showed them all the disparate flowers of the field and weald, and was nice to them, and shared his snack, and wanted to take their snaps home as a small momentous, with their two shirts off in the clearing ('Come on, sunshine, you don't mind us seeing you're chaste'), which Albert did and Mr. Chinn politely tightly wouldn't. They left him at the crossways, waiving their chary-o, and swearing themselves to scare-crossing, though nothing had happened, still they had in insight some sense of danger-view, of hanging by a threat, a treat of sedge and violets.

Even when it rained on Mr. Chinn and all friends, and brought them dripping in, or when the evenings drew them in, still there were playing places in the neighbours' indoors,

36

musky lofts and higher attics, bare boarded rooms that were beyond the run of the house, like inner ruins or left apartments.

Already then the map of Mr. Chinn's world contained its little known continents, its darkest freak apocrypha, its Africa, its unexposed hinted lands, its romps and swamps and runaway terrains, its asiatica, its aquatic arboreal far easts, its forbidden tropics, its quixotica. All red on the map was the known and sunlit world, everything under the thumb of a victorious blighted umpire. But beside this groaning upright world there was for him an unread unknown unlit land—virgin terror-story—an uncharted unshirted contrary where, though he was not a native or a genitive (expressing possession), nor was he a missionary, a mercenary. Neither one thing nor the other, in or out on either side, he was happiest down in a dump, where he felt himself delightedly not at home.

PARTIAL
TREATIES

There were special collusions throughout their year, trips and treats and partnerings, when the family peace would join together in a grin, and Mr. Chinn and Sis were at the centre of a tension. On sunny weakened days the rug and the rolls would be outspread in a clearing in the bracken or the beeches, on the shingle or the cliff-top, handing round the orange sandy wedges, the ginger cake and pop, and the chocolate picnic-biscuits, whilst everyone played ball. There might as well be headlong day-long drives down A-roads and low-roads to see old formerly friends and neighbours, the Wisemans and the Shepherds of yore, and parley politely with half-estranged other children until it was time to set for jelly tea.

At half-time Dad would take them, the père of them, up to

the mews or the zoos or the mausoleums, to towering London's oohs and aahs to see the sites, the clanging of the guards, the doom of the unborn worrier, the crowd jostles, all the faces at poets' or speakers' or the lions' corner-house, the vulgar square and the chamber of harrods. There was always a choose and a piccadilly sandwiched in the park in between, and time to feed the orang-utans and the lemmings. Then they were driven away homeward in the darkness, drowsing in the back until the last stretch and the mutter comes to a dead stop.

Once upon a year, with what solace the muddle of summer brings, their double-bluff day came around for Mr. Chinn and Sis, with an elaborate tease and party-crueller games—pin the toil on the darkie, hurt the thumb-nail, pass the arsehole, blonde man's blush, and the fireman wants a whiff. There were canticles with the cake snuffed between them at a single blow, whoopee worth-day to double-you. Dad would show them up later, turning out from overwork to be the clown in the middle of their last tired giggling ring of cheers or having them in musical stitches, until it was time for bye-byes and dads and mummies came in drives to correct their children ('Have you been gored? What do you sigh?').

In the dark shadowed gallows of night-ember time, they would gutter together around the burn-fire on gay folks' night—bangers and smashings, bun-puddings, treacle and pops. It was then that Mr. Chinn first felt the licking of the flames on his hot fleshes, the skin-dilating fizzling sensations of playing with fear, a love of the world of nights and fieries.

And then the windier solstice brought charisma time. Grandmother and Father Chinn must pay for a visit. The door would be ringing with postman's knock and heaps of cards and quarrellers singing astray in the major and sharps come wailing in. The shops all fooled to bustling with crass massed dreams and crass massed presence. A vista for Mr.

39

Chinn and sister to the santa panto classics or to the exulting encirclements of the spinning big-top. On crispness day itself, after seeking in stocking-feet and the hope-pining of well-ripped particles, they would all sink down to dinner: turkey's delight with all the crammings, chestnut-cracker stuffing, plump padding all aflame with Grandpa's best banter, toast for the clink and keen, and Dad pouring round and round with the wine, accepting all those who uncles and aren't too tiddled tee-hee already. All of it too much for tiny tums, with nuts and humbugs handed about. All of it too touchy for grand upsets too, with a good old family ping-pong before the night is through, or a hot punch thrown in rancour on boxing day. And once all of them huffing out of Grandma's house in a blur, in a bluster, in the middle of a game of snap—letting out in one expulsion all the pain pent up in happy families, the outbursting of the boil the balloon.

At all events, both birthday-parities and customary-fastings, Mr. Chinn would sit in dazed glaze-eyed wondering, gawping at the glum fascinating flicker of the candles, and thumbing the velvety tassels of the undercloth one by one by another one, listening to the passage of laughter along the table, the pausing after, and watching the openings of teeth and gums, the fillings of mouths with stuffings and nonsense. Vacillating rhythms. And with a finger on the cloth, or with a sparkling writ against the sky, he would begin to fill in, falling under the spell of words, words—words in the head that were plucked from the passing flow, and plumed and penned without constriction, without even inking. There would be would-be perfect words in this slow secretive underhand way, write perfect words, beautifully scribed, the only perfect, middlingless words he was ever to know.

But for Mr. Chinn it was being ill that was the nicest nursing treat of all, the most illustrious, made him feel precious and cured for. Still wittering his writing with his fingers' ends, lying in his flushed white sheets, he would hear hushed voices and steps bringing him up a tray, a toy, a tea-cup. Sitting wanly on the plump fevered pillows, a jar of mucus-aid beside him, with his weakly german muscles or a touch of fluid, he would enjoy a snuffed doze, play games, even when he was two weeks in bed with jack-in-box, itching to be out. He enjoyed the sensations inside his body, having his temptations taken, the whole wriggle and roll of being late up. When he was older he would give himself a good thrilling, uncurl his supine, stretch and yarn, enjoying all the lying there, the loosening of feeling in his limbos, never wanting to be willed and well-healed again.

SOMEWHERE HOLIDAYS

Once a year they took off, everything and everybody, packed up tight in the back of the old moorish with the biscuits, the blankets and spuds, all their stocks and fishnets (every year it was everything bar the christian sphinx). Swinging singing down the old Bath Road, the trunk-roads, laughing to the B.B.C. beside the seaside, loving to go a-yonder with a gnatbite on my back, and full of glee of fol-de-lee to get there, and to be the first to strip off everything running down to the sea's edge, shouting and jeering last one in's a sausage, panting and waving, and in quick amongst the chill thrill waves and whoops and jumps for joy. Every year it was like this everywhere, taking leave of their sandals for a fortnight, too weak with surfing with surfeiting with sunning with running to know whether they were

42

homing or glowing. Down they went whistling westwards, ho-ho-ho, down through the nirvana dorset, through sunset, through the rich red earthly devon, and into carnival, or the other way to wassails.

For Mr. Chinn bliss was it in those dunes to be a loner, and to be hungry fairly often. He was lost in complete openness, climbing on the sole-destroying sands or the ticklish crusted rocks, escaping from anemones in the pools or sending secret sea-words in battles. Always here alone of anywhere he was his own hero, his own caruso, his own crusader. He lived crouching over the wet sand, making mounds out of molluscs and shell-stocked castles in the mire, or domes and dams and finger-meeting tunnels, channels, his reddening soldiers burning in the sun. He laved it in the sea, the ease of sitting in ooze at the sea's unsettled edge. It was perhaps the memory resurfacing of bath-night bliss amidst the surf, the oneness and wetness of the all-surrounding sea (no man is an I-land, all alone, but he can wish himself a happy isthmus), or deep happy nappy memories of sitting smiling sinking in his own slime stink, his own dank bliss and piss. It was his pleasure to stand eyeing the meeting of sea and sky, the blue unending blending and oblivion, his orison, his plea. And even going to home not-home, the little tinny abracadabra-van, with its lifting seats when it was time to turn in for beds, and its tables turning out of walls, this inside-outhouse, this magical box, too was pleasure, palatial, playing at living and sleep.

He loved as much as anything this simply being bare, the unfaked near-nakedness of every body. Perhaps what always kept him growing, what funnily made him goon, now as in his afterlife, was the design of returning to such a prime evil state, a para-diddle dice-all chance of innocence in a sense. When he was his neutered natural denuded self on the shore, he was almost Adam in wonderland, gone down to the sea to breathe—no longer Edom or Eyesore, losing his birthright to the promethean land.

43

But when he turned his back on the sea, the one-duck sea, the latter, he always fell, fell headlong body-longing as any unaided Adam always falls on the uneven strand, unable to stand himself foundering on the sands. Through his sea-bleared eyes it was his gaze that fell, fell lingering on bodies not his body, not his scanty skinny thin white-skinned streak of a body turning red, but on tanning well-toned browning beauties, baring their August bodies to the beaming of the sun. These were the sea-serpents, the sun wash-uppers, washed up on the beach, lying low admist the foam, Dune-Apollo's children. In summery shorts, they were his first attemptings, the first flickerings of the ur-virginal Chinn, but not yet the lust. And with all this still swimming in his blurry eyes, whenever he went to the public pool, Mr. Chinn was always tempted to touch the bottom, for which they often threw him out or in.

Left torn between the burning yearnings of the shore and the flawless flowing of the sea, he made his pitch, his patch, in the wormy uncertainty between the tides, the unsure. He joined with the scum and drift, the wrack and wreckage and weed, the open broken shells. In this untidalled litter with his finger in the sand—as on the loose edge of the cloth, the sheet—he wrote his name in spiralling letters, his wasted words, and signed himself in sand in feigned defiance of the all-defeating, all-obliterating, letter-hating waters. Sent tuppenny-ha'penny coastguards too to nabobs and relations, relating all their doings and throwings, and ending with the usual feeble fibs: Having a wine-dark full time, Which were you where, and, Aches mar the spot.

JOHN THOMAS: OR, THE HISTORY OF A FONDLING

When Dad it all began, when exotically was it? At an age of before sex, certainly before he could say nine thank you. At about eight then, about the lasting stroke, eight or more of the cock and all swell. Bedtime betimes, and little Mr. Chinn all ready all tucked up halfway down on the slope to sleep, slippers beside him, his unbelittled corded colourful bahamas on him, a new check drifting-down on the peg. So much time spanned in this closeted cosseted way, doze and yawns on end all addled up. In the little room with the cottoned cross-bowed window that seemed to swell and swell and swallow all the room and him up into its vagrant outsize darkness, into its crow-black craw, as he fell afloat.

And then in the quilted quiet the hand on the knob and the

eye-latch softly stirs in the door, in the darkness, and opens. In stealth in steals Dad in silence for a last hello goodnight kiss. No alarm, all warm in that. Mr. Chinn rolls over to sigh nothing, breathing sleepily deeply. And if there are words mumbled on Dad's hairy lip they too are sweet soothing mutterings. But on his breath there is the sour city smell of his grinning and chronicling, his too many just anothers with his friends before retraining home. And if his footing in greeting stumbles it is nothing serious, but why perhaps his bristled lip in passing brushes the bare beardless cheek of Mr. Chinn, the fair skin, and seems to pause there. And why he takes his weight, waiting in this gaping chasm or spasm of a moment (was it ours or yours or only belonging to seconds?), palm on the pillow fingering a strand of the fallen hair, pressing out a starshape of shadows, and why perhaps with his free hand (free! the all-constrained pre-ordained doomed left hand) he fumbles with the sheets, fumbles and finds the dark warm opening, finds and fondles the fair-skinned flesh-thing in his hand, handles and dandles him fondly a while, saying nothing, nothing to say in warmth and darkness, in depth and weakness—nothing to be unsaid or undone until the whole while is just passed away, the hollow wile played out. Then on tiptoes, fingertip on lips hushing him into unspoken silence, slips him back into sleep, and creeps himself briskly out of the room.

Just once or two or maybe three times this happy unhappy unjust happened. It was all that did, not much. Or perhaps all that ever did in the hole of his life, all that opened to him, mapped out his life there ever after, hope-inning door after door into room after the same small darkened room forever with the same scene unseen plied between two between layers of the darkest of innermost darkness, the same players, the same pleasure and impatience, the same por-tents, same unimportance, the same lack of meeting, lack of meaning, the same hopelessness. The same feeling fingering

46

lingering, same longings. Never now to leave his father's house, his manor, no escape, no door bolted, only every door leaving you black into the same black room, over and all over, and all the same you lack room, hiding darkly, no scope, no escape, only waste and repeat at leisure. The same cosy, the same crazy, ness. Here the seek-rutting, scarred life of Mr. Chinn begins, the single pattern, beaten over, in the dead of night Dad infinitum.

Then when later he relieved all this, Mr. Chinn began to think it had not been, had only been dreamed on the farther side of sleep, infant-sized fantasised, a wishing a meeting in his mind only, the fervid forbidden. Then he truly knew himself to feel only and alone. No flesh of his flesh in bloodheat mingling, tingling. No touch or tickle from hands other than his hands. Nothing ever now but his own unending unbefriended frig-mentation, the days and nights of his own self-hating own self-hunting, his dick-end little john peeled, with his hands on his horn in the morning. This was his gorged god now, his idleness erected in his own imagination, his scrotum pole, his penis mightier than the sored. Not to be sired and desired all at once, he was left out on a loose limb, limp, fatherless, futureless, faithless, face-less (Who killed cock-rubbing? I, said the spoilsport), seeking out in vain for ever after the one-defile warm-handed blest molestation he had known and never owned. Never owned up to. Never braved a word or spoke about it to a soul, a spook, from that day to this.

As for fathers, forgive them for they do not know, what they do they too do not own, they also are alone and lorn and quick to the touch.

GREAT SPARTAN MOMENTS (Number Two in a Serious Issue)

All during this piece of time there had been a bout between the worlds. Between two great hemi-pyres a conflagration of the sense, between their first divisions an almost equal match. For most of those longueurs it was a time of waiting uncurtained in the dark, a time of russian capons and stale meat, with nothing happy paining. Sometimes a point, a hit was roaring scored, and in the echo or the mail it could be heard reworded for days or miles around. But whose or wise or watch it was never tidily clear. Too many ghouls and own-galls and no-guiles to be sure. All's love all in games of warfare.

For Mr. Chinn it was half-hearing lying the nine o'clock noise, the booms dropping and the droning ceaseless hum and dream of will they get you too. There would be midnight alarums and excursions with Sis to their daughter-and-a-son shelter, down under the stairs with dressing-gowns on trip-toes, all a bit like christmas leave, with Dad or Mummy standing hovering saying don't diddle, no need to picnic. Waiting then, half-a-doze at six or seven, for the yawned dawning and the hall clear.

For Dad and Mummy and all the groans it was always talking it out of them, standing opinioned to the garden-wall or on the fence, a leak of notions in continuous motion, saying to themselves and their hob-nobbers what it was and when it would be all over and all but finished them off last night, next year, send us to christmas come. All of them listening in to the priestly intonations on the warless, learn-ing to haw-haw and to jaw-jaw well.

What it was all a bout of Mr. Chinn clearly never knew. Certainly there was the leader of the naafi party, Rudolf Antler, Rudolf the rat-nosed rentier, satan with his slayers. It was tanks to him we were at war with the shermans, and all at sea as well, trying to get our envoys through against supplies attacks, using up all our stubs in the sinking of the teutonic. A fight to the finns against them. Down came nasty Rudolf across the plane-fields of east-end with all his finns flapping, his laplanders landing, his norsemen nastying. Blew them to blitz.

And standing firm against the antlered herds were we, the anti-stag parties, only we, wee chilly winkie (two but very small) and quite a few. He it was who told us all, chewing on his sugar, 'Never in the quest for human comfort has so little been sewn so far, so there.' And we all had to go out and knit for victory, make more artificial arms and legs to clothe in on the enemy, make vest-fronts and warmonger-wear to keep off the cold stealing in from their pantie divisions, make flag-jackets for flying in, pairs of sheets in come-off large sizes, or jumpers with boots and belts and bronco. After a palaver, the yanks were there in ranks with their pullovers, good fighting chaps. There were canadian monties getting caught in shorts with the desert ratatat, seeing off Oliver Rommel at the battle of El-Allemagne, and piles of poles and fleeing french and austere aliens flying secret emissions over the bilgings and the ditch. Even the rusk rations were with us, all lies.

In the end there was a bidet on the landing to relieve the french, parakeet droppings all over the place. Then there was marching to the tunes of starving berlin, ivan's a fellow, and our own dear the divorcee's sweet tart, a violin playing, 'There'll be blue blood ever' and the biggest hit of the profiteers of doom, 'We'll make a gain'. Finally they were all shaking hans across the elbow, with dances and hangings and kith in the streets, the victory prates, the glib orations of years' hopes. Our kin and our quaint (their mad jesters) wavered to the krauts on the balcony of beckenham palais, and winkie puffed again what he had always puffed to keep our spitfires up, and sang to his huge cigar, 'We shall fight them off the premises, we shall fight them in our living-rooms, we shall fight them in the hall, we shall never serve reindeer'.

This was as match as Mr. Chinn never followed. Standing not understanding at the tar-marked edge—he always kept his difference—with the sandals, satchel-bags and sandbags flying past, he would watch the daily deadly worry-games run and acted by all his others. Their fights and teemings made them all ready to be candidate cadets, their boy shouts of you did and codger and rules of packs repaired them for the life of force. They were filled brain-full with all the mixed piebald-school idols of sport and saving faith, hymn-singing and he-man training (scrum, psalmody and the squash), turning them win by win into muscly christians, emasculated cretins.

When Mr. Chinn saw all this straggle, the shy shining grin of the moment's winner, the heavy body's golden-haired hero, then he would feel all his own feeble, all their fabulous, his all alone aloof, and their lively foolish, ness. He did not joy in their spats, their sports, but this plague-round was the world, he had already caught it, been taught it, and already he could not complacently take his turn away.

KEEPING MUM

Then saddeningly one day Dad was gone. Lived out the war unarmed only to be overrun by a car, a traffic case. He was only crass-crossing the street, only to boast a lesser. It was his own fault, his own feeble slip twixt coupon and collapse, never reached the post. Trunk of course, dead. Had been going round the bender for most of an ill-thought night.

They brought his loosened grim grimed body back to the gate, Mummy beside himself. All of it they hid from Mr. Chinn and Sis, the collapse, the corpse, the arrival of the cops, the unbalance, the bawl of the bells. It was best they did not see the full measure of misery, Mummy instantly falling to her knees in an attitude of players please, and unstintingly snatching back knocking the scotch-bottle in full measures.

Instead they were sheltered off to be sent on jaunts with aunts, to be taken in by grands and friends' parents for keeps, with treats and sweet-smelling pillow-sleeps in unfamily rooms, taken away from themselves. Death was to be swallowed up in frippery. There was between them then a simper that was a solace, their small solder stiffened, their hearts hiddened, against the forced out gales of false laughter they had to bear, the fabled jerks, the destructions of all kind, all ingenuously intoned and tended. They were kept away from the coffin-mourning of the fumarole, the music on the wail-less drowned up extra-loud, and Mr. Chinn could only hold in his mind's sigh a picture of boxed bodies sinking slipping and sliding this and that away into the flare, the fumes, into the sitting son, the re-cremation. Everything up in smoke, hushes to hushes: return to cinders, Dad's dross unknown.

And then when they got home all was deferent towards them for a day at least. Mummy was clammed down now, and on her own roam more and more shut up. The bed had been ridden into the corner, the curtains re-drawn, and all Dad's clothes put out. The last ties gone. He had been quickly cleared, cleaned out, sponged, his picture not anywhere to be faced, so that in time even to Mr. Chinn it dimmed and finished, bleared and fainted, became a dis-remembered grinning at a distance of smiles.

The news was broke. They were poor girl and lesser brother now, almost awful orphans. All a loan from now on, debtor and sum. Dad had left them everything in his bills, everything he owed. Mummy was plunged into meanness with her mourning, trying to keep in the black. All harmony, all her money, was quickly gone. It was to be penury-pinching and pass the money from now on, everything wearied and gambled over, every last panic to be accounted for, Mummy ceaselessly dolorous over the extra vagrancies of her charges.

She wanted to be a well-sustained classy widow, a wife on the asian way, a package to India. Or at least to take a boat to the canneries, to the highlands, to somewhere dearer and drier. But the widows' cruise was always full, and she could not ford it, she could not fund it in her inheritance with all her little mite. She had to make do with a witless week in tin or pawn or yawn-mouth, a wrong eke-lend in easter-born, or an off-seaside spell in long-dead-now (always the last resort). From which she made her annual returns speaking nothing but ill of the debt, of all her fellow complainants, all her feud, and saying how she was broken now, how she couldn't passably go on, how much they were going to have to hope and skimp and slave.

And yet as Mr. Chinn himself was launched on the slippery way, he paid not too much noticing to all of this. At least he preferred to sink himself as a ship off the old dock, rather than carry around forever his mother's cheapness on her childer. This was what he tried to make on his inheritance, his father's empty quest to be. We watch him grow out of it with simple interest.

STAIR
CASES

Everywhere there were steps that had to be taken. Stony stairs in the genial and the signior schools. The first two times that he tried to take them twice astride, like the big boys in their dilatory two-step, rushing steps, done at a bound to impress, Mr. Chinn missed, tripled over his footing, and fell on his face. First contempt of manhood this, and not the last miss he took, not the last fall over his own defeat, not by a long chump.

There were as well winding secret spyhole keyhole stairs spiralling into the towers and spires of no-man keeps and gothic catacombs, up into the skylit safety-railing air of châteaux at their windiest, rook-circling castles, places of magic and lost majesty, dead lords and ladies. Mr. Chinn could never step foot on such a stored-up shored-up stair of memorials without a sense of tread, of the ghost-head being clear ahead of him, the silent axe-man waiting on the next turn. But he kept himself going, something inside him kept him incited, his eyes full of the pitch, the patches of startling star-bright light. His ears would be attent to every cling and lowing and ecco, be held to the thrumming within, his skin alert to the lightest touch of a single skein of spider-spanning, his nostrils thrilled full of the scents of danger, the mangled smells of moss on mould and dust and the piss-offerings of many. To all of this he gave his guarded ascent. It was the same in later years when he was doomed to stray down into the maladied mildewed marvelled halls of public cavities, with vessels and scurf at his side, the same trilling together of aye and no, the same certainty on the stairwell that will was given over to must.

And in his dreaming all this time there were other flights of fantasy, like the grand gold ballet-room steps he could descend to general réclame, to a hush in the crowd and three admiring hussars—he would be a jewelled jowly rajah, a grand imperative or an ex-sultan, a singer-ella or a glorious swansong, making a lasting entrancement.

There was too a dream of stairs that was a scheme of careless daring. He would find himself stood at the top of his own home stairs, thinking himself not treading not climbing not walking those stairs in the usual careful one-time way, holding the left-hand banister, nothing sinister, but cheerfully rather flinging, flying himself off the top into air. Dream of a happy landing in the hallway, no falling, no failing, but a perfect sweep, a swoop, an arc, like what a lark, dreaming himself wings.

But in his undreamt-of reality, there was the time that his bestial friend, Albert, for no apparent resentment, pushed him from behind from the top of the precipitous tearaway. How odd, ow, god, thought Mr. Chinn on the way down, finding it painfully clear as he stroked each raiser's edge and landed on the bump, shaken, stressed, an unbroken fall, that he did not, would never fully understand his fellows. Their chums and harms and japes were always going to be a mixed bliss to him, part come-fought, part hostel.

So it always was for Mr. Chinn: against the endless failure, the dream of unending free-fall, the flight fantastic, the crest; and against the dream the dark allure, the crash. He could not ever quite leave either of these alone, so that he was always left hovering between both stories, a grumbled dupe of yore, neither hope nor drowned, fatally floorless.

In all the long son-forsaken days that followed his passing father's death, he would be sometimes found at the stairs' foot hearing hello low talking in an upstairs room. One footstep up and it was unclearly his muffled mother's tone calling long and dearly on the phone. But a call of what nature? Two more quiet creakless steps creeping higher, one rung up at a time, and Mr. Chinn could strain to hear the talk itself, pricking his ears to pick out warm words and half-heard heart-felt phrases from the flowing, but not the whole, not the whole-hearted secret reason of his mother's hidden lingering. It was only one foot more to know farther, to know fully his mother's privates, her hinted mates, her seek-rites. But he never did. He never took it, as a rule, a private lore, never took the next step, but stopped on the half-hearing step and held himself on this side of the thrust, the truth. Stood on the ledge of the knowing of good and evil and did not entirely fall, did not untimely go up. He couldn't face it, and he couldn't leave it alone, but stayed on the line between, the bother line.

All was confirmed, converged, one day when Mr. Chinn stepped through the front door back from school and into the damned undimming light of the clarity that begins at home. Next to Mummy, in his Dad's replacement, in his father's choose, caught hand in red hand standing, stood a half-stranger, a half-familiar, a bigamous man with the

57

demeaning friendliness of a grosser, smiling with a pipe in the clench of his fist, and a smoke-stench filling the flushed air.

'This,' said Mummy, in her best and phoniest darling-tone, 'this father, darkling, is going to be your first step.' Mr. Chinn could only stand and stare.

A PASSING
EXAMINATION

Was this the stare that broke the family pack? That clinched a thousand slips, lunged a thousand mishaps? The lost roar? Penury for your thoughts, Mr. Chinn, penny for the gaze.

He knew even then, oddly enough, that something of nothing had happened, that something basic, mental thunder, had broken inside him and there had been a shift, a rift in the foundering equations. Perhaps he had joined the traumatic society at an early age, but this was the first time he began to get any notices.

O there had always been his older elegant other, his antithesis. And in his father there had grown to be the strong and distant stranger, the clinging constant cringer, almost the kid. But now, standing in his eyes, there was yet another, one father further, the new surpasser, the usurper. And next to him, in Mr. Chinn's kin and keener double vision, was the new due plasticity of she who had always been one to him, one over all else. Oneness will ever cease. And if she was no longer single, what of him, what of Mr. Chinn? If she was lost, how could he any longer be won?

He was not King Camelot, nor was meant to be. No great dominus, no great dane at all. More a little noodle, a whinnying pooh, a petty thing lying on its back wanting to have its yummy suckled. He was no great eros. Naughty would never happen to him, no great avengers, no swash-tickling advances with the furtive region, no in-bush jack-cades with the marquis, with the jack-beanerie fighting the ogrish argus for free, for fraternity. He would have acquired life, that was all.

But what he had now real eyes for, was that from his retreat he could watch himself, his unsafe self, go out unscathed into the addled world, into the wild. His pugnacious, trusting, scar-jawed double could go about and dabble, watched from in hiding by receding Mr. Chinn. He could be two without any trouble, double-dare himself on the stairs, let his feet and fingers follow his whims, his wish for warmth, take a shit in the dark, and come up smiling of ruses. And he would watch from the stillness, unmoved, with his unblinking paralysed. The lessons, the licence, of his dream lurking-glass wet-patch cindered dark-room drama-world were not lost on him. He was the expanding pupil of this privy close-room, which stood him instead in good unsteadiness for the future.

So his pretentiousness began. Facing a shattered, scattered, repaired life in an unfathered nest of his kin, Mr. Chinn decided to live only on his own turmoils in switch a world, to live at one remote, playing himself apart only by pixie. He would recede into his own tiny mind, his own little words of his machination, and take his little dogsbody for a walk, to exorcise it, only when asked by the calls of his nature. Thus at last he took cleave of his genesis, took league with his fancies. Left him a cleft Chinn.

It said as much at the end of his final turn, in his last riposte, when all those who had ganged together to give him a head time, a hard start, matched in one line to say of him:

Mr. Chinn has been wrecking in all his classrooms throughout the year in a highly certifiable way. For all his skilful skull-shape, his slack and fugitive appearances on the field have been a mutter of concern. We cannot really make him go out at all. In many ways he has been a cordite to the school, and should go off with many surprises at any moment. We wish him all hell to break loose in the furore.

SPECIOUS DAY

The extinguished guest rose to his fee:
'My lawns, lanes, and cheltenham; your preference;
dead martyrs; voids. Uncostumed as I am, I see from
where I stand today that all of you sitting there are privy-
legged. I see it in your faeces looking up at me. You will go off
from here to lead private-ledgered gilt-edged lives in the
sold-out outside world. You must not feel a shade of this.
There is no knotted wrong in our privet hedges. Here today,
we have salivated the beast among you. It has been my
treasure to present the bribes to those of you who most desert
their honour, to those who have come first in the fallen
luggages, in mystery, fast in the acrostics, in arthritics, worst
in the seances and in litter, top in craftiness and munich. The
point is not only to give all a few their duress, but how the

rest of you will go on to make loose of your alibis. I might as well say to your wall: use your talons, use them widely, but use them for the general bun-fight of satiety.

'Some of you in term to come will be bleeders of industry. A sum of you will join the processions of the sylph-like serviles, or of the lower or the medium sins. Some will be solos, sages and pirates in his manifestly one-armed four-somes. Scum will look towards the knowledge of our coldest universes, and lead the life of squalor. Orders will go into things wholly other and join the charge. Still utterers will seek to be erected members for permanent and to win the corridas of power. I hope few of you will be good in spurts, and perhaps reprehend your country playing crikey at Lourdes. In all your works of life it is who you bereave, and whatnot, that mutters most. Maybe it's because I'm a landowner that I love laying down the lawn. But remember what I say, what if you do, and you will all remain wealth-wielding city-gents of Greater Brixton, and humorous old beans in the sight of Godalming.

'At another time of year we recoil from those who weighed down their wives during two weird whiles. We murmur their selves of senselessness and their carnage. From the going up of the balloon to the chopping down of our sons, we will dismember them. But these same vultures have their value in pastimes too. What I say above all is stick to your princely pals, and that way you can come to know ma'am.

'In clothing, I undress myself peculiarly to the smaller boils. I was a boil once myself. If I am such a cesspit now—and I must be or your gunnerers would not have imbibed me here haw here haw, a little choke—if I am some chestful now, it is because I have hallways and kept in my bed free drinks. Thirst, be trite to yourself; sequinned, be a trial to all those who lie on you; turd, and venially, be a truant to your cunt. With these simple ruses in mind, you cannot help it, but farewell.

'And now, in collusion, I ask you to provide three chairs for the covens of the school, and I ask them and the bastards who touch you all so much to grunt you all a free off-day in the voucher. Whip, whip away.' Lout jeers, followed by a pause.

And so it was that Mr. Chinn made himself available for highers, went off with all the bruises, shook fists all round, gesticulated, and laughed his dumb-brained schooldays behind him. Law, distrust us with thy bossing.

IN FRENCH EYES

Took his leaves, and decided to rest on his laurels, no longer to resist his lorelei awhile. Cursed his mother good-boy on the platform, packed and ticketed himself off, got out a booking for the journey, and sat in victorious excitation waiting for the first shunt the first jaunt of the night-train, the jehovah-to-calvary crossing, all the way to ferry-land. It was his first time aboard, the longest adjournment.

Arrived at his destined station ('C'est magnifique,' he sighed, 'but alongside Waterloo, ce n'est pas le gare'), and plunged himself into the micro, the macro, all the scope and scales, the chasms, of city-life forming in front of his eyes, the stray whiffs of gallic, sharp wine, and all the sewer of their pressed bodies in his eyes. He sat and smiled in his all-ajog corner at the faces around, shapely noses, dark and full hair lipped and eyed, salauds. He knew how anguished, how angular he must look, that britons never never never shall be suave, and felt come over him in waves his first deep love of far-in far-awayness, the golden ego-laden mien and all the clamour of these creatures, these parasites—enfants de la patrie, du paradis, citroëns de la république, republicans and seigneurs.

He settled himself into his shabby-genial widow's pension in the letting quarter, took in the view de la rue from his balcony state—one old bag-lady with a loaf, two priests, three marketeers, forsaken dogs—and then went down and out into the square in a state of one-deux. He had eyes for everything, city eyes, capital eyes, and walked himself around and around ceaselessly. He had his trifling tourist eyeful all the time, up with the arcs the parcs and down the champs-élysées the musées the églises. He would look at the pictures in the livre, the mystery-pieces of the Vino the Mono de Mimosa. He would walk along the bois de belong with an inner pensive air, catching the romantic fever, the reverence of a foreigner's solaced air. He would find himself frankly broke, and get to the right bank in time to change his reveller's cheek. He would cross over for Samaritaine, determined to return like his duty-free arm-filled father, full of the gifts of the bag, a grab-it-all son. And after such a day, enjoying the streets and narrows, he would sit on the Quai d'Orphée following his culture-odyssey sipping cocteaus, supping his carafe, his café, his head growing round in a span.

But at night, some other smothered emergings came to life to grief. The den-city lit up its rouged alluring lights, its promises of cheap-show thralls, of quick excess. It was all eros then, all tingling with its open offers. Nighttime and again at night, without thought without fail, Mr. Chinn's steps drew him to the streets, to the well-worn cravings of the pavings of the Boulevard de Cliché. It was for him a taste of freedom this comfortless pulsation, this compulsion. His worst anomie drew him to it. He huddled himself into the rhythm of the pacing crowd, his mind bent on all the implicit pleasures called up to mind by all the shouting touts of the demi-monde—paris-eyed and mattress-eyed. He heard of scarlet pimps who offered whore-kids, twelve or thirteen at a time. Of houses of ill-repair where there were exotic intertwinements undertaken, share madame and share masseur (or vice versa, or worser vices). A borrowed hell-hole manned by skin-diseased siamese, where you could experience numerous vile asians to your person, sadist factions guaranteed. There were certain curtains behind which mirrors showed the merry buccal bacchanal of unreflecting couplings. And booths where youths could be abused or amused for a few moments soothing sous—mise-en-cabine, infantilist regressions.

He would ask himself, but do I dare, do I dare set fate in there? And hold himself at bay, almost spilling with despair. Then one day he took himself in hand, and hanging round the usual blue lingerie shops, the strip-teaserie, licking his lips, he made the plunge. He pushed blushing past the door, the change within his grasp, and picked up a delicious tart——a tarte aux pêches, he knew it was a sin.

IN
INVERSE CITY

H e had been so far down that it was time, full time, to go up. Fall, in fact, season of misfits and futile melodiousness—o yes indeed, the heady camphored uxbridge air was heavy when he arrived with the pungent plangent strains of unlaundered lovelorn under-grovellers singing to their small catarrhs in smaller hovels or student-infested garrets, songs of limited youth and undying trying ardour.

Mr. Chinn was up, fully-gowned, in full possession of his faculty from the moment he entered his first Q.E.D. wrangle with the lay magicians. Strut away he found his feet, his tongue. Mr. Chinn up early for a run with the boozy-figured dons, or for a turn on the water trying to make his punt come clear. Mr. Chinn up late, still arguing the tussle, the gloss of their flossy fizz, baring their candour at both ends. Mr. Chinn up to his hours in books (o he was shelf-indulgent throughout his leaf). Mr. Chinn up in charms at all the mabels, all the mary may-king, rolling out the double-barrels, never left fleeing soirées for himself for a moment. Mr. Chinn well up in all the latest newest fangled notions, the news, the novelties, the policies, the poets, the votes, the photo-finishes, the visions.

He was half-way on a stairway of his own by now, still tittering on the bringing into the college of good and awful. His newfound friend—an ami or enemy, for still he found his french-apes, his copains in shape amongst his least apposites, his opposites, his fiercest revels—his latest cleaver, clever Bruce (the jolly juvenal malingerer, the master piss-taker, burly lascar, scholarly wag, Bruce Campbell from edenborough) was a flight above him, on a different plane.

Together they went to all the lock-jaws, to all the poor festerers to hear their prefacing, their endless prolix hums and hahs. The top of the cant, the leaders of the oxen at that time, were a muddly crew, putting descartes before the hordes. There was A. A. Eeyore (the weeping fool-officer), Lewd-Wit Wittenberg (the laughing fall-off-his-chair) and Bar-Trained Arsehole. There was Boris Burner (who couldn't tell his labials from his balliols) and F. R. S. Hovis (who couldn't tell his arts from his alembic). And Lazy Daisy Thistle teaching sweet M.A.s, and St. Moritz Bow-Wow solicit-dating the classicists. Bruce and Mr. Chinn went to them all, and spat at the back in the expectorated fashion, making their asides, their dawdles, sneering and snoring at the herd.

Their evenings too were spent in moots and mutterings. The cry at that time was all flibberty, for eternity, frugality. A publican spirit reigned. Orders of pints were taken first, and then the gender followed through, with bitter attacks and stout defences, reelings from the chair and the motions

sickened. Until it was closing time for any other baseness, rose to their vetoes for a lasting chorus of the old red rag to a john bull, the old landlord's sign, the anti-rationale—and then out into the strides, bomb-raiders armed-in-arms wailing home, fellow-trivialisers, harmless arm-sharing revel-legionaries. They raged in their beliefs, from the heart-over-head pacifistic pussy-footing Christian socialites (who swore by their Bibles, Engels and Bede) to the hard-headed fisticuffing foot-stomping unquestioning red-star linesmen (who stuck on their marks, to their own sects, and did not let go). But each of them, whatever ails, were all aggrieved in the single-minded causes of universal suffering, ham-rolls for the connollys, and an end to the borgias' state.

In all the cross-talk of their theories and theologies, whether at party-nights or amongst his own classes, the whole wise words or otherwise of Mr. Chinn flowed and followed ceaselessly. He chatted the unknown shallows of new notions, and talked his quarrels with in-density, he and Bruce in deep debate, baiting each other's lines of ergo-you-meant with fresh whims and sharper harks. Each in his corner sits and takes his stance, decking out his whereas, his saleables and sybillines, tricking out his oracles with arguments anagogical, historical, metaphorical, metrical and pre-hysterical—falling into goggling fitting laughter on occasions each at his own observed absurdity. Whole nights of indeterminacy were passed like this, with not a thought of bed between them, filled with budding ideas and bidding fond adieus to the two bodies of unspoken knowledge that lay beyond them—each marshalling his epigrams and covering over his fallacies with codding—preferring both in this reified atmosphere to obstruct thought than to conquer it.

So what did he learn in all this time, what did he gather that gave him his disagree (a bachelor in parts for life, gained inner second)? It was nothing he knew. He had it all read and known before, at tables in bed on beaches, or sitting in the tweedledee gardens as he knew it now sitting twiddling his dumbness looking through his french tutor's windows onto the mellow-aired jardin: that language is arbre/tree, an autumn never-static churning over of new leaves and dead wood, that he would never groan out of, never have a wreck-mended route for, a mantic-parlous raillery that he would never race in.

LOSING HIS
FRAGILITY

On the night of the congratulation-ball (it was his end of part one, as he later reckoned it), Mr. Chinn was taken aback aside in the darkness by an insisting sinister hand, would not be left alone. O he was tight all right squeezed with his cummerbund into that dark corner, and the summer band wrecking and reeling—two-step, fox-trot and stickily under there—a sham pain fizzing in his head, hands unbuttoning the dicky, his or another's, a tongue swollen inside his mouth, and a breast pressed breathing hard against him.

As it took its primal course, through to its brief bleak conclusion (major promises and moaning grimaces leading to this sullying jissom), Mr. Chinn found himself loosely idly thinking, So this is it, this is the monument we have all been waiting for—erected in honour or offer to the great god-king, Sex, first of the love-birds, father of hallucinate days, all-wise dishonour on our minds. Having done his dribble, dislodged his dibble, he thought it was an end of all his trouble, when it was only the start—he should have known it, catching himself on a fastener as he came away, squealing with all the appearance of passion as he jerked himself free. Master Beaten's number-one rule of naughty jug-jugglery: First, don't catch your hair.

And yet when he came to himself the next day at noon, no-one still there, hungered and overslept, he could not even be sure with whom or what, into what party or holy or divine orifice he had committed his sin of emission, his venereal peck. It could have been a well-endowed linguist (French and quick with the Finnish) who had been lurking her lap at him all evening. Or it could have been a Very Importunate Persian, for all he knew (there was one in the college, son of a shah-holder). Or it could mirrorly have been his forevered immer-negation, his always no-body love-me. Coito virgo sum.

It was at about this time he opened a book on himself, to make himself a better, made up his own account, the first of many, entering it all in his moments of ledger. There was much in the debut-column from the beginning, bad habits, old sod-its, a morbid audit all the way. He counted up the cost of his lost teats and teeth and curls and curdles, and weighed up what had gone missing with his fear of high water and of the dock. He had nearly lost his marbles once, his conviction of marvels for ever, in the play-grind. The age of mirror-calls was almost gone. He had lost too his tremble voice, his nerve, his sense of parlance. He had lost his faith, his face, his inhibitions and his ambition. He had been lost many times in admonishment. And now, to tup it all, he had lost his virility, his vile-ability, he was no longer a self-continent, a pure-isle Chinn.

But in the other calumny of his life, on the incredible side, there was only what accounted to one sink-all entry in the book to cut his losses. You could hardly say he had won his spurts, or his slurs. But he had now for life something that could never be a token away from him: he had the high price of being himself, he had won his in-depth penitence.

MR.
CHINN
TOO

IN
VACATION

O f Mr. Chinn's first dipso deviance, and the root of
that foreboding fruit-tree, see in Reynold's Evening
News (or other peddled organs of the playable gutter-
purchased press). You'll never get that trashed in me.

Meanwhile, o for amusing fare, o for a maze, a fair that
would astound the Brighton and Hove of inversion. O for a
muse well-boozed and mellowed at the Pierrot'n'Asses
watering-hole, one over the eight.

This was what he doddered in the holidays. Often he was
inspired, in spirits, listened to the voice of his inner double
daimon, his scotch mystic. Sometimes he surpassed himself,
passed out entirely. Or walked along the prim modernity of
the front with all his frantics, all his peers and supporters,
well-peed for paddling in the puddles, all lit-up, ill-

humoured, ill-mannered, shouting out their melody, their malady, their worst, at the tops of their vices to the passing puzzled crudes. Bruce from below bellowing out his abstrusenesses and obscenities. Chinn and croneys, poems number-one, handles in arms. He nearly knew that he was only wallowing in his father's foot-staggers, time coming full sickle, sickly, the second-hand. But he tried to make it out that it was a farce a phrase he was only pissing through, a stop on the way to somewhere or else.

Then for a dutiful son-loving day he would pop and soda up for a visit to Mummy, sat and brewed over tea-pots and plum-jam whilst his stop-gap father pruned and pottered in the garden. She would pour out and reminisce to him all the while almost to herself, remembering news, nieces, new dresses, new addresses. When something was let slip clean out of her mouth, she would call to Daddy through her half-open widowhood, forgetting the dead Daddy, the which, and bring her head in flushed and flustered, reaching for a light for a moment, a smokescreen to cover her harassment. He would come in bootless a moment later, piping something between his teeth about his daily years or his crush-ants or his collies.

Later she and Mr. Chinn would resemble, would resume, skating over the thin nicenesses, the links the rinks between them both. Saying how sad she, how bad he, how dare, how disgraceful, how unfaithful, how mean—meaning your father, always *your* father with a meaning glance (your father, witch-hunt in heaven)—how low he had been, and then as soon unsaying anything, everything, with a little laugh, a little toss, a demure little look, if for a moment Mr. Chinn hinted a demur. 'Of course, I don't mean,' she would then say, 'no need to get on your high-pitched hoarseness, my direst, my dulling.' And adding, 'And when are we going to hear that you have settees and eider-downed, and put a wife over your head?' It was not that she was getting on or past or

78

her mind failing with these little feints of hers, not at all. It was only that in the despicable unspeckledness of her lounging life, the unspeakable spick of her entire span, her husbands and her habits, all the clutter and chatter had been removed to the corners of her remind, to some cut-off lumber of her loft behind. Minutiae, inertia, adore a vacuum-cleaned home.

Or he would go for a lengthy lunch with Sis ('We like to see you fed up'). Sis, of course, was marred and married now, of curse, to a husband dull and shady in the expert trade—something frightful imported, by all accountants—with her own drive and detachment all obscured, absorbed, into a fresh ripe legacy, a replica, of their own mothering. There were two kids, nice enough niece and nephew, who roared and careered around him, making him their favourite jungle. But in all their sports and the piping racket of her smouldering husband's high-financial hi-fi nonchalant noise (he had taken an instinct dislocation to Mr. Chinn, and usually turned up his noise at him), there was no longer any spare room for Mr. Chinn. He looked for the good look of old, the bonds of the girdled days, when they had been insuperable. But all he saw was how far got-on, how far cut-off, this has gone, and Mrs. Sis.

And so, in low relief, when some are gone, he returned to baseness, back to his stair-studied life, his fellow-revelling with mauled and bitter brews, with Bruce, his loan life on easy terms.

Tell us Leo, goggle of mystery, muse-guider of his story, tell us as the start-signs turn, the stern sighs start in the fundament, tell us all, lie on and on. What augurs, and under what influence, in what consternation, does Mr. Chinn return his heathenly body to the universe, his overdue looks to the bodily library?

MR. CHINN'S WEAK

B y now he had a settled day, a rooted-in routine. He was
like this.

He would awake at sixes or sevens, his ears pierced
with rings, and stretch out his alarm to switch it off, turning
in on himself and over for another forty flighty fifty wings.
His sleeping self, curled into question, was still his deepest,
his least profaned: a homage to catatonia, morpheus in the
wonder-world (trancing the can't-can't), punctuating his
days with a coma, a semi-collapse, and this fool-stop.

Then with a new poor power, gruff, he essays anew, yearns
loudly, and faces himself if he can out of bed (drawn by the
old mirror's dream). Drowsy the curtains apart, fisting his
eyes on the day straight ahead, he drags himself in search of a
light, a tea, a pot, the morning's toilet and the paper. By ten,

by then, he is washed and shriven, razored up and trousered, not without having jammed his daily bread first into his great full gorge (new every morning is the loaf, thank crust). Mr. Chinn, up again, and rickety for the world.

At ten-furtive he is at his books at last, de-suffering their sighing non-efficacy, swatting little notes in the well-thumbed margin, the migraine of truth-seeking already welling and thumping in his head. The conscient rationing of his thwart-filled brain lapses, collapses, and on the stroke of leaden, he marks and vacates his place in search of a coffin for his deadened, beaten mind, a tiffin, a brake on his prowess.

An early lunge with similarly exerted friends at any of their round of hubs, speaking an inflammatory deal of nattering, rude barbs between gossips, and perhaps a gamble or two of arrears, why-are-yous darting between them with the cribs. Time like this after time dallies daily in the back of the so-long, stands distilled another round, shame again, until the balm-man calls it time and quits.

By gone in twos and threes, Mr. Chinn and his chronics are labouring again under the library's disillusion, pawing over fol-de-rol editions, and stretching octaves, and dewey-decimos (the old foxed tomes), or taking notes or a nap, until it is time to slip their desks for more critical crosswords and four-across tease. Stuck in their commonplaces, gassing over their mediators, warring themselves spread out in front of the cross-fire, now their non-stop nonce-topical world-play really begins, their fierce-eyed chats with hot blistered toes, and crumb-bits, and blague arrant shams.

They were still at it, daggers drawn, stilettos over the dinner-table, jangling all the nerves and forecasts, sometimes dragging on till dawn, chewing the facts over whiskers and ziggurats, cheap liquored-up loquacity and babbled inanities of nebulosity.

And all for what? For Cuba, or for other sites of sorts of revelation. The end of cloned rule, or the adam-bomb, the

81

abysmal-tomb, or the deafness of God, the mute-ability of man, or the nurture of art in this post-irrational, post-Hiroshima, post-Auschwitz, past out-witted shattered age, the need and security for cobbled unionism, or the neat obscurity of cubism. What's cubism to them, or they to Cuba, that they should quip and whoop and have a whip-round for it? The subjects of their nightly jousts, their lists of passionate concerns or fashionable stands, were not their object. They needed however to loosen their vowels, to exercise their lingos and their diagrams, to keep themselves in fits.

It was the same for Mr. Chinn at the senator of all their parleying, all their trivial tribal deep hates, as he raised himself up on lofty pinions, swooping all before him, ready for flight, flight and flight again—I will descend to the depths, you're right to say it, he would admit with a revolted air—like all the wrestling of them. But somewhere still inside himself he set aside a settled, sceptical side of himself that did not belie, did not bluff or bleed a word of their spoutings. He held himself a little in reverse, joying in all their bouts about whatever, too voluble, too feeble to resist, but knowing that there was apart from all them a part of him that was not real lies, a self that came alive in lying down, behind closed certainties, closed eye-lids, an idle id that came awake aware in darkness, away from all their wordy goods, and started stalking when they had finished with their talking.

If this was mundane delay-time living, choose day was no divergent, and wends day went marching the same bored route, with perhaps a weighty ledger to fill in an hour of the mourning. Never a day passed by when he did not give himself up almost in tired release to the doll-dreams of his day-dramas.

Wanes day far into the night he was, for once, not boozy, but busy under his head-lump, riddling what he should have

82

been rid of long before, fetching up far-fetched turns and parses, writhing his hearsay for his terse-day truth-torturing, screeching with his nib, his head, for the nub of what would be his I-say, scrawling on all forewords, never knowing how far to keep his claws in or out, in his crabbed writing—hoping for some language, some parole, that would shorten his sentence. Up all night, all lone, to get there.

No wonder, then, that the next day was thirst-day. Spent all of it, his hard-learned dash, making pint after pint, putting across his high-brewed potions, sinking on his feet, until they finally led him out cold and got him to slip. Frail-day, free-day, was hardly headily there at all, spent all his time under cover, not over-hungry, hung-over, with an unawaking head and belly.

As for his sadder and shunned days, his weakened self, how was this spun out, how did they pass muster for Mr. Chinn? In lingering, in laundering, in wandering talks and walks with friends, with brusque ambles into the off-beat tracks, with Bruce Campbell up to the hill-tops and down to low, lying, perished churches. They would finish with clotted ice and crusted teas in samedi-thatched weekenders' cottages, and, as a rule, a well-thumbed lift or the last bustle home. So the sundays of time passed away, and Mr. Chinn returned to his work-days, his shirk-days, his so low life, his endlessly repeated monodies.

CHINN
IN LOVE

Something had to hamper, to break into the monogamy, the stuck rutting, of his life. It harpooned at a party, at a meeting. He was there with Bruce as useless—brazen Bruce forcing himself to the forefront, into the fray with his hectoring, his chuckling from the rear—when he caught a glance, a double blow. Bland Cupid's blundering dart from his stupid little bow had struck him down, doubled him up. He looked impaled, his hurt rent to its cubic root, so that even Bruce, braying his asides, asked him what was the martyr.

'O dear, o bruise,' he said, a longing expression already on his bloodless lusting solipsism, tears in his sighs, 'I have failed in love, fallen in laughter, at first sigh and with second sight.'

'O crutch,' said Bruce, 'what effing has marred you to do that?'

The answer was a leman, it always was. Mr. Chinn had seen her on the fair sidling of the room. She was a blonde, high-grade, tall trull, with the bold shoulders of a freeze-style swimmer, an all-imperium goodly meddler, the thick thighs of an athel, a complete athene. She had a contrary air in her ruddy cheek, the rude health of a pharmacist's daughter, a fine upstanding kine of a woman, six feet in her stockings, all butt. He was cowed. He glazed upon her with amatory amazonian self-abasement.

Her ice had met his, melted, cauterized his solitude, his soul. Seeing her had seared his heart, sealed his unvoluptuousness with a loving crush, speared him. He was hooked, looking, would not be spared. He asked amongst all his allies who she was, and was she wooed. He was disparate to be in, to be traduced. They told him she was Valkyrie Allison. 'But you,' she said, offering him her hand in a mirage, giving him the right, 'you can call me Val.'

And then again, on the other hand, in a half-littered corner of the same hall, was another, an idol yonder brother. He was a small neat, an eight-stone worldling, black-aired, lustrous, dusk-eyed, long lashings, thick, clipped in his accidence, flashing every ivory tooth when he lifted his inflected laughter, and sharp-suited in the loudest fashions—white-eyed and dark slick blousers, wilful scarlet shocks. He was a mogul-he, a supple simian, a dark force, an out and out-sider, a far-runner. Mr. Chinn had known other ecstatic exotic spacemans in his teemings—venturers who had stepped from the dockside of the main, from other distanced plantations in the garlic-sea, from beyond the urinals, east of aden, from the land of nimbus-rodrigo, the land of nod, nighty in the shade. But this was extra-spatial, this one was moorlike. He would not ask to know, he would not dare to speak, his name, his norm, his gnomon. He would keep him in sacred as his antinomy, his nomad in an island, his mad-friday, his mephisto-kid, his privateering diversion.

And so Mr. Chinn was caught and cut and torn between the two, doubling in this magic, doubting it, not knowing which and who to turn to. In all their party-calls, all their cries of down and up with this and that, he must contain himself with long longing sighed-long glances. When they were chanting long live thingummy, he was taking his chances with the long thin loveliness of one or the lingering lithesomeness of the other.

There was no hope of a quick coming-out from his courting of come-on please. It was only in his deep-riven mind that he could steal a kiss from both of them at twilight, crept, osculated, corrupted and oscillated between them in their slumbers. He could only keep himself in check with words, with a verbal warbling, his outpourings of seduction, his powers of diction. In this way he redressed his ballads, addressing himself in hard lines to his mistrust thus: 'O Val, your face is oval', 'It meets with my approval', 'O be my Val-entwine'. And to the dark laddie (Mr. W. H., Mr. Who, Mr. Why, the only bedwetter of these insanitary pursuits) he addressed himself inversely in the pursuing sonnet, spun out of the yarning of his word-web in which he was cockaigned, ensneered, and tossed off the loins which began: 'Shall I compare thee to a Saturday? Thou art more lively, and less temporary.'

GOING
DOWN

And then for Mr. Chinn it was all over, the place was
ready to go. He had obtained his degrade, the onus had
been passed onto him, his batch finally examined. His
books were boxed, all his processions truncated. They had
sent him his purpose, his join-up letterings, cancelled his
leaves and called him up and down into their world of
unnatural service, of notional face-saving. He would serve
his team, his far king queen and country, as he had been
brought down to do, his wretched men. His hirsute days were
over, suddenly all cut off. His chaste, pure suit of Val, his
shadowing of his black-amour, were all up-ended in the new
chase for valour.

Whereas Bruce had been led off, had fallen into a lucky
fellowship, saved himself with the quality of his stud-ease,

his deep resurges into the Furry Quim. Bruce's historico-so-so-eco-gnomic work on Marx and Spenser, his high-marxist doctored theseus on the effluence of the Defined Commodity all over the sonorities of Apostrophe and Scholar—later pulped and bleached as a booking, *The Beatrice and Sidney Web* (I.O.U.P., 2 guanos)—this was the base of an arcane-craft career, his entry into arcadia, into anaemia, into the ivory-towered rivalry-powered world beyond the pale, the pally-safety, from which Mr. Chinn was cast down. From here the patter of their pair of lulled lives diverted, and each went their desperate ways.

Yet not for Mr. Chinn the shit-brained brownshirts of the infanticide. Nor the streaming-cold guards changing their bare skins in front of the populace. Nor the unruly knaves, the mercenary navvies, the rowdy maroons, going down to the sea for chips. He joined the little blue boys, the Real Airy-Fairies, the riff-raff.

At first he quietly injured the barracking and sport and punishing, the hours of sick-bay training, mocking time and shunning the commandments. He, from his smothered sub-barbarian origins, had never known before these the rest of the crew-cuts, the recruits. They were his welders and betting-men, these bull-necked anguses, these georgies, welsh-ape toughies, tattooed cockney cockatoos, with whom he now shared their debunking, their crudities and credos. He, with his inkwell-bred accidents, his broad folk-cabbalism, was outside the wrangles of their true thick unthinking, their grunted this and that, flunked there by a sentry feudal force. And so he was the butt-end for their revels, the object of burly slaughter, their jockeying. But it was also him they buttonholed, beholden to him in matters of fact or friction between them, in letters to home it may concoct. And so they went together from the cor-blimey to the meticulous, they got along formlessly.

But all his dream of flight, his journeying whoosh for the

white-blue wander (why d'you blunder?) fell flat on its force. He wanted to be a piety, a prelate, a high-friar of the heavens above—not a low-padre, a right charlie chaplain, but the real amen, a sky-jumper.

They made him sit pillion in a chip-monk, take a ride in a trainer. He couldn't wait to get his fingers on the juice-stick, fully-throttled, deep and drive and yelp and yare. And when he yanked at it, taking control, the country rolled, fields fell on him from all slides, he dipped into a dive, swept into a swoop, and nearly brought a yankee pirate in his spare strangled bomber out of the skies. He could have been the star of a new-world war. It scared him weightless, sinking in the fracas of a suction that it was his last, his loss, and feeling blunderingly for the call of his paraclete in case he had to loop. But the pompous pilate whisked his hands off him, and saved them both by a close whisker.

Then when it came to his mediocrity, his ridicule chat-up, the M.C. slapped him on his back, tapped him in jest, listened to him with his telescope to his blighted ear, and pronounced him unfettered for surface, unfit for flight. He said it was his poor breeding, not his accident-prangness, his unsatisfied lungings—his M.O.'s bare-faced motto was, 'Poor lad you are. Had asthma?' Mr. Chinn was groaned, grounded down, a landed janitor, an unrequired lubber for life.

SEWERS'
CRISIS

B ut then wince again, there were war-sores and woomeras of warriors, rumblings against the pacts. The Pry-Monster was on the waves at all times, reinsuring them all in unsubtle unsettling tones that all would be well, well, well. Pepper-rations were being made, sandcastles bagged for sea-defiances, our fosses were standing soldier to soldier in already éliteness.

The saturation-point of it all was this. Some foreign baddies, cryptos, chaps, had struck themselves in the meddled east in the feed-pipes of the waste. The drains weren't running on time, there were shits blockaded for weeks in the kennels, and the whole of the untreated mess threatened to spill out into open whiff-air.

The streets, the wet cloths, of Dover, the states of gyp-

royalty, had to be kept clear for vassals and messuage. The dykes and the ditchings and the duchesses must be freed, the manor-hall covers kept open, the manuring-system main-drained. There was consternation in the press, four-inch headlice told the story. There was constipation too in the House of Commodes, talk of the whole gentry going to rat and ruin. Digestions were laid down by vulnerable members, motions were passed. Never since the days of the earlier cess-pit, the first earthling of Shat'em, had there been such offal scenes. The cabinet was in ceaseless occupation, the privy-concealment sitting. The war-lords too were up in aims, belly-grossed and bilious, making guttural speeches about how we beat the germs before, how we wouldn't be swamped now by some frightful froggy plague from the faroes, by any general nausea or dirty nawabs, or by their commie-khazi pilots. We'd blast the gutter-snipers out of their hideous places, we'd flush them out with every last dropping in our arsenals (there'd be a handful of W.C.s in it for the most careless, the brazenest), we'd loosen our barrels all over them, bomb-hole them to smut-marines. We'd guar-antee them strafed conduits, we'd whip the offending effen-dis out, the imam-blighters.

And Mr. Chinn waited, wearied and wary, knowing full well who we was when they said us much, sitting in his bare rags, treasures round his anguish, waiting for the call. Once more down with the breeks. Ordures would be ordures if only they came, and he, with all the others in the airy farts, would be down there with them, the Queen's Irregulars, the Filthy Foot, the Turd Refusaliers, mucking in, if the missile came, the ardour to shambles, came winging through the ear-waves from a wireless in Gaza.

And soddingly, sobbingly, in all this broken plummeting, for the first time he, Mr. Chinn, Fluent Offencer Chinn, Flaying Orificer Chinn, saw clearly his own future death-feet before him, his own red white and bloodied corpse hussled homewards, and all the others, air-maled back by the last post. And not just him or them, but the whole bloody lottery up in schmaltz down to the last drop, in this new unclear warfare. It was not funny, no jakes, it scattered him skitless. In this, the diarrhoea of a nobody, in the midden of the campaign of his life, it was a darkward obscurer self, where the dire echt way was lost. It was a churning-point, a millstone, a heavy waymark.

AROUND THE WORLD (IN A HEATED DAZE)

It was then, emotioning his name written rotten, all in scribbled garbles on a tomb-bomb—imagining their moans will live forever, their numerousness will live on heather moors—it was at that monument that something grave gave way inside instead of himself. He founded himself beside himself, with fear and fury and foreboding.

But the cull never came. In its dead, in its wake, there was a half-truce, threats and treatying. Hurriedly was the inkling of it, the incongruity of it, on the paper tried, when Mr. Chinn received a posting-card for far-run parts, for him to go and show the flagging spirits in another's corner of the glib. It was then his wanderings, his nighttime red-light errings, his me-and-her stirrings, began in earnest, in near-east farthest parts and ports. He lost and found himself all over the place, in all the torpid tropic seaside shanties of the horrid torrid zoo-towns, all the lecherous hot hells of ex-attic cities.

From the mouths of the Tigress and the Youth-rapers, and all the perfidies of a rabies, the deserters' sunderings and the deadly sea-skulls, to the furtive cross-hunt; from the farthest tent of the Ptomaine Empire and the Holocaust Land (he went to the wheedling wall and had his profit picked in gullingly), to the easter shores of the made-it Iranian; from the walls of destroy, the toppled towers of Elysium, from the Athenians' greed, the hill of the metropolis, the mound of Olims, to the pay-again cities of Chi-ro and All-asunder (he thought of Clio-patterer and the idolatries of March Antinomy—the chi-chi satin in a varnished throne, long finger-painted niles, the snake in her grasp, the chic of aberrations); from the ancient enchanted city of Carnage (where dildo and an anus strophed in love, and their ghosts still roam amongst the runes), to the ruins of Rome (the Severn Hills, the Colossuseum, where all Rhodes lead, and the ancient Forum or against 'em); from the farthest rickshaws of Well-hung Kung and Seeing-a-porno and Bang-a-cock ('You are Mr. Sin,' said the gay shy girl with the kimono eyes, the Tokyo Rose by any other name), to the shaven wonders of the nude world in Bonus-houris and Really-did-you-Nero (the low-cut neckline and fall of the romantic empire); across the pan-American Cannibal to the fastness, the immense-cities, of the yes-you-oy-vey, the U.S. of All-Meretrix, on and on through Knew Whore-Loins, New Jock, Lost Anglicisms and Sun Sin-frisking, with yet more gambolling in the cassandras (again he made no prophet) of Lost Wages in the Nerve-hardened deserts, playing his Texas in the Loin Stir State—in yet more cities of the sands of wistful time, more cities of the pharaoh-plane, ancient and modern, indigent and maddened, new and old Soddens, unchanging Sordids, Gomorrah and Gomorrah and Gomorrah, with all the creeps in these pitied places from day to day, here it was that Mr. Chinn amongst them all passed out his time.

In all these satieties, all these pleases, when the hot and tumid power of darkness downpoured, and the swollen moonshine uprose, heedless hatless hot-headed Mr. Chinn would steal from his fellows (an oat or two), and follow his scent into the bars and borderlines and basements and even more bizarres of the city slimes' scant scandals, its candlelit hide-quarters, its gutterings, its melts and shambles, its goner-rears. Though he knew that quaffs and sleazes spread diseases, and that cripples who lived in doss-houses shouldn't trust loans (neither a bar-fly nor a wanderer be), yet once he was on the loose and on his losing streak, feckless and fantasy free, whether alone or with his crazy gangrene, he was loreless, careless, callous, and lost in gay abundant. As soon as he had stripped off his uniformity, his regulation blues, and put on his muffler, his shifty look, his night-untiring search for libertine bodies, with an unclean hankering in his pocket, then he was changed for the worst. Then something wild and wilful welled up inside him, something mucky, mocking, not quite clownish. He was a scaramouch, a savager, a runt, a hunter, a hanger-on, hanging around the bin-backs, hungry for pickings, ravished by all this rubbishing, a dog, a runaway flea—what he had always been in civvies since first he was a paris-ite, since he first learned how travel burdens the mind.

MR. CHINN'S DOUBLE

It was here and there, amongst the droopings and the dreg-addicts, that he met his matching, discovered his personal pair-version. He found he had an altered ego, a double-yoke that he had both been from the startle, from the moment of his twinging birth.

O there had in all ways been such another, searching out a nether rejection, a reaching, for them both, an unholy twinning, a tweedledee. He had always led a dappled life, a double-cankered assistance. From his first thirst, faced with a double-breasted suitor, he knew whoever secure he was, there would always be an udder. He found himself afflicted in an upending row of distraughting mirrors, the unfair ground of his undoing, his upbringing, his downfalling. And so it was at harm or abraid, there had always been a second hell-thing, a little drivel, a demon-strutter, an imp-affection, to show him a better bitter badder way, a squalid route of all evil, the dark side of the man-in-the-moan.

But now, for the forced time, it had a name, a ludo, a shadow-anonym. It was Mr. Egg, who joined the forces with him, who enjoined him now in his night exorcisings, and went far about ahead above him, keeping him in the dark, urging and eagering him to keep himself up, egging him on to his face. It was Mr. Egg, and Mr. Chinn was nom de plussed, non-plumbed.

Messers Chinn and Egg together were mess-mates, chief mismatchers, mischief-makers, piss-instantly in and out of tribunals, often in hot waiters, or seen concertina-ing with the caitiffs, sometimes taking absinthe without leave. Mr. Egg was the wag who was tailed by Mr. Chinn, the bright-tied and pushy tale-teller to whom his headlong heed was paid, told him what haunts, what hunts, what luck, what larks. Most of their Egg's-appearances took place in Egg's-dreamily Egg's-pensive settings, in an Egg-sultan in-nabob-rated state for which Mr. Chinn always fitted the bill.

Mr. Egg was the devilish willing dervish dancer, the wild-man who had drawn the in-a-spin Chinn into his heady swirl. He was Mr. Chinn's companion and compulsion, his boon, his bone of incontinence, stain to his folly ('That's another mess-fine you got me into'), adding fool to his fear. They were fellow-lurkers together, liars in waiting, the town-decriers. Mr. Chinn knew every unstoppable step of the way that it was an Egg's-perdition he was embalmed upon. It would lead to harsh Egg's-changes with his friends. He would be caught, they weaned him, in the fire of a military cross Egg's-ammunition, an Egg's-quiz-it Egg's-assize. He would face Egg's-communication and the threat of Egg's-termination.

But Mr. Chinn had soiled his soul with him, soldered his solitude onto him—they were detractor Falsehood and

Metro-sophisticate, docked ejaculator and mistried. He could never bring himself to Egg's-hurt himself, however far Egg's-aspirations brought him down from his own Egg's-posed position. Nor could he entirely Egg's-placate what his Egg-sight meant, or why he allowed himself to be Egg's-taught in this way, why he was such an Egg's-silent pupil.

So who was this Mr. Chinn's much vaunted (vaunted dead or reviled), vaulting (and again revolting), faulty (to whom he owed his fealty), haltered Egg (a fabled yoke he had to bear), o who was he, this Mr. X? Was he a rank-and-filer fellow-officer, a naafi-sir, in Mr. Chinn's battalion—a pet-ally, a platoon friendship? Or was he poorly a disfigurement of Mr. Chinn's emerging nations, a mirror-age cultured up by his feathered brain (is this a daguerreotype I see before me?), a hollow-sedation, an allusion? Or was he rather a sure-thing soothing credible alibi, someone to pin the beam on (someone to demote in your own ire), a good Egg's-accused for bad behove-you, for all the flings that Mr. Chinn wanted, the great to-do that he couldn't? No one new, that much at least was plain, an old unknown, an old familiar, like Albert and Bruce before him. He was Mr. Chinn's insuperable patterner now, that was sure, but who he was was a Mr. E.

CHINN OUT, CHASED IN

Then, at last, there was an end to all this prompt and proper pride ground-down trodden trooping, this mad marching, hair-trimming season. No longer did he have to stand it, a wrecked, correct, cracked up to be what he never could, at attrition or a tease for ows of drill unending. Mr. Chinn, formerly F.O., bashfully B.A., frigger-officer and basher of arses, was out.

He had had his discharge. It was inevitable, no effort at all, given his dozens of bad egg ways, his by-ways, his buying of any goods or bads in any stew or stall at all, any flesh and chap shop. Although he always knew it was a strip-off, he could never resist a bar again, or a little cash-sex, a little nightie clip-joint where, for a couple of pounds of flesh or a few thousand leerers, you could see nipples and dine.

Given all this that he had taken, everything that his wage of life had brought him, his being an immodest vendee, it was unenviable, sauna or litter, that he should be contracted with a dizzy seizure, something he had picked up cheap, going for a snog. It was a good buy for all that, adios of the collapse. He was rewarded with a preposterous post-humorous V.D., a voodoo, unbeatable for value, invalidated out of the force, and given a special treatment.

Then he was back in Anger-land. He was let loose, unchanged, on Skivvy Street, on Scurvy Street, bob and jobless, home and hopeless. He went down, skunk to the bottom, as fasting as anything, foundered himself hungry and slipping in dark alleys, by elementary canals and cold stark cul-de-sacks. He spent broken slummers, dossing and taking turns with the worst, on loaned makeshift mattresses in dread locked houses, and wittered sullen nights away on the depraved streets with cold, long under-bridged nights spanned underneath the urchins—sleeping on the flintstones with no pay. From dawdle to dust he walked the crazy pavements of the sluggards, of the stubborn and nothing sides of the reviver, old father Thammuz rising from his broken springs, crossing and recrossing himself at Hunger-can't-afford for Charring, at Foxhole and at Backfires, or even at the farther ex-streams of Depth and Dirt-ford, and the Trés Riche Monde of Cheers-Wick and Queue.

He got nothing, no work, but only weaker and weaker week after week, no lodging, no largesse, no base, no basin he could call his own, but baser and baser, even driven to filching the odd clean sock, the little knicker, from the public broth-house, the soap kitchen. He would stand on an empty stamina staring in through the steamed windows at the full butchers, the bakers stuffed high with rolls, with choice and briskets, and at the candy-stick makers, stacked with their farthest riches of chock-full and crammed trophies. But he was having none of it, hardly even a rumour. He

100

fell backwards, whenever he had a bitter to spare, or something turned up tramps, on his oldest cider of labyrinths, his old shrill whine, an unthinking drinking injudicious spree, dregging himself in Egg's-horribly to another surly grave—bier and skeletals. Which left him adrift alone again, nothing gained, the odd copper on his empties, on his tail. He often evenings fell back on the chary shared teas of others, of his fellah-men, and of the dogged do-gooding ladies, the prig-aids of the swill-ration, the starvation army. He was chastened into hostiles, imp-hounded by the ill-met at moonlight, by the meths-row plodding police, carted and discarded off like a stray, like a destroyed dog. This was what it demeaned to Mr. Chinn to be dunned and routed, to be downcast and outcast in parishes and laundrettes, in Erith and Hendon.

Now he was in the dying strata of society, in dire straits, in Queer Streets, why did he turn his back on the aid and betterment of all his friends, of Albert and Bruce and Co.? He did once phone Val, only to discover she was engaged (and there was not even any flirtation to her reception). But why didn't he call out for Mummy in the night, for a banker's draft, for a couple of wads for Christ's sake, something to tidy him over? Or press Sis for a loan, a single or a double-figured check-up, enough to get him back on his fees? Was it that he was afraid to ask the question, in case (like, What's life?) it turned him back upon himself to the pillory of assault, the wreck-ignition of his own fool's start? Or was he afraid to be obscene in their eyes, to face their fussing, their forcing or refusing him? Or was he simply a frayed, a threatened bare version of himself, an unwelcome remainder, a laughed-over?

IN WHICH MR. CHINN FIRST GOES COMPLETELY TO PISSOIRS

In these disparate streets, in the sheer cheerless sharing need of his loinless life (a nasty city is the mother of inversion), Mr. Chinn was first driven drifting dripping down into the dank dark-end stinking stagnant unsettlement of privates' light fantasies in public levities, in feigned-hearty jakes, the trashy tragic comedians in puzzling convenings. He joined up with a dread carnal army of the dregs of regular sojourners, on the night pit-roles, their in-descent into the wallower depths. He knew it was a poor way of making friends meet, but in his paupery, in the pot-pourri of mixed-up types he met there, the wrong foundlings he fondled at the fountain, he knew whenever he had two pees alike to rub together he felt a richer wretched man. He knew too he could not have met a bitterer glass of poison anywhere, but still he had his passion, his penile servitude, for a habitation he could not cack, could not handle by himself. It was yet another part of the cause, the kiss, hounded down upon him from father to son.

O he had always had an enticed taste for tile-lit places, for the dingy odious dung-laden male-odorous air, the pooled and pushed and puddled doors and floors, the involuntary flushes, all scents and non-scents, the cracked pots of the stales and sinks. Since his first night-marvelling of stairs, or perhaps before he had taken the first steps in his self-containment, to hold his own amongst the rest of them, before his too-late training had even begun, he had always felt himself at home in the pits. It was a favourite rut, a fervent rite, of his, the making of a mass amongst his peers, the laying on of hands, the shaking of the waters, and the blessed release of the sunk-excrement of his confession. More than once he had added his own pet-urgings, his own please, his gravity and effeteness, to the laughtery walls, and sat back in some saddest-fiction that he had left behind his mark, his muck. He had come to settle there for good or ill, a joker in this house of cruds, this shack, so that much of his life was passed fallen between two stools. It left him with an anchoring for the gents.

And now, with the effluence of Mr. Egg upon him, leading him on, letting him in for it, he was the boggy-man himself, the pick-up trickster, one of the pack, one of them, the candid fruits, the weirdo-twanks on the look-out for a lad in his genies, with his pantos round his wicked ankles. He was the fairy sod-father, prick-eyed for his closet companions. Before he had always minded his peeing and queuing, his own business, and washed where his hands were going. But now he was on the prowl, playing with his stealth, desperately kneading, always keen on the outlook the outcome for likely-minded others, old codgers, younger brothers, and avoiding the dangerous thin eyes of fellow-voyeurs who were troubling in his direction (people who needed peepholes were the yukkiest).

He knew all the most futile haunting-grounds, the lairs of self-deception that were involved: the dun-johns in the park, the jims, the saunterers and the showers, the most freak-wonted bars, the station water-loos, the cock-towering wish and brush-off. He knew too all the rules, the ruses of their games of patience, catch and shuttlecocks, the rubbers of wistfulness, the in-tricky steps in their non-men's morose glances—and above all their vows of silence, their shut trapped trappist monadic existence. He knew too well the brief enchantment of these counterparts, the clichés of their clinches. He knew the reeks, the risks he was ruining, the little chance of rescue. But he concluded that it was better than nil, such tangles, better than no-leave-me-tranquilly when true-quality never came.

In all that time, amongst the others, he went with these: an underchef from Nuneaton, a choirboy from Hassocks, a spotty cockney youth from Hackney, a lavatory-attendant from W.C.2, and an old queen from Purley. There was a young labourer from Limerick, a persistent suicide from Leamington, an ageing juvenile-lead from Oldham, a shot-putter with well-developed pectorals from Chester, and a snap-shotter with well-developed pictorials from Ilford. Also a tight R.C. seminarian from Ethics, an ambitious young executive from Korea, and a more than able-bodied rear-commodore's son from Crewe, who performed fellatio and a half-nelson on him admirably—'Kiss me hard,' he said, 'and call me hornblower.' 'All right then,' said Mr. Chinn, 'you've twisted my arm.' And every time he felt a little badder, a little less haunted, a little more wanted (if only by the local johnnied-amorous, the bobbies and the men on the off-beat). But he was never quite caught redundant, and always seemed to have to get a way with him.

TEACHING
ANGUISH

And then out of the sky-blue, his lark scuddingly began to change, first signs of the summer or whatnot. A postscript came from old bright and Brucey, the old card, from his new college where he was a junior don, a don jaunty enough to be a danger—still he had his whiskied waggish way with whimming and words.

The latter found Mr. Chinn on his uppers, on a downer, but it brought him the hope of embroilment, the chance of a connection that Bruce had got it made. He put his best suit forward, the patched-up harassed weeds he had always had. He put Mr. Egg behind him for certain, Egg-sponged him clean out of his mind, and went to be vetted to be viewed by a small bald bilious tyke, a tyrannical old concupiscent sorcerer in a low-browned study. This was the damned dreaded dandruffed scurfy scruffy squeer-set thickset head of a preposterous school, all false gravitas and thrift, a crammer-school of the worst, the highest feasible fees, the lowest passable pay. It was a lowly lonely hardly enough kind of a job, but poor buggers can't be cruisers for ever. Despising everything, their lack of felicities, his look of inexperience, Mr. Chinn took the offensive and the offer, and cadgingly accepted their half-terms.

Soon he frowned himself back to scowling, to scolding, it was all he could do. He was put in with the lower filth and with the upper froth, the scum; they gave him the horrors. They were not all wild boys at all, not untamely ripped and roaring (apart from the hardened corps of them, the cads and cadets), but rather a herd of cackle, a giggling of fowl guzzlers. It was less of a black-bad jungle jangle, and more of a chalk farmyard, with a band of pipers forever crying out loud his sir-name without sir-cease without sir-ending, and a susurration of discussion, of scuffling, whenever he passed amongst the desks.

He was implied to teach them the king's jingles, inkish litter and languishing, to train them in the grimmer points and finikier rule-ways, and cram their class-sickened craws with sweet William's Sharp-spearmint flavoured thingummies, give them the works. But from the look of their blank visages, they had no test, no comprehension, for the turgidity of Helmet facing his own Dane-nation, nor for old O'Leary and his dotes, nor MacElizabeth and his hits and missus. And it was no better either for the second-best bards, for Worst-Word with his whimperings loonily as a clod, or for Grey-beard's Energy in a Chertsey Cunt-Yard, which brought them to jeers, or Gravity Browning's Nude Goose (bought from C. & A.). They were not even half-appeased enough when he wanted to give them all a good dickens.

The trouble, the tribal conflict, lay in the fact that Mr. Chinn could not count the roll, could hardly con the droll or keep a straight lace, no fabled Able, he, nothing like. Sometimes he left outright, laughed out lewdly when they bruited him without abatement, made him their butt-end and shown-up. Once they were compliantly jeerily silent for a day, which made him almost ill at their teasing. Once they ran so completely a-mocking, he had to fetch help from the staidest twitcher on the staff, the head of martial and would-work. And once they completely turned the tables on him, sat backwards in their desks to him, and then he couldn't face them at all.

But at least for all his labouring education, his carrying the torture of learning, they gave him the run of a house, a rough and a tumble over his head, and a drink-home of some ate hungered poundings a year. It was a kind of sick curacy, a means of assistance, a job's comfort.

STRIKING
LUCRE

I f his imp-rovings had already begun to come to an ending, now it seemed they were unending in themselves. The next throw of the never-say dice brought him a winning fall, a won in a thousand bit of luxury, the cheery luck of a row of cherries that lifted him into a full-life clover-field, into a new living, a new river of leafiness where he thought he could put behind him the cloven-footed forecloser on all his detours, all his pliabilities, his defaults.

Mr. Chinn met a traveller for an antiques firm, who said, 'Two vast and lidless trunks stand in your potting-shed. Mind if I take a look?' It was a coffer, an opening he couldn't refuse.

What it turned all out to be, once it had been sought through, and most of it thrown aside, amidst all the clatter

108

and low junks, all the crocks of ages left for mess, the many old irons, the rugs and bone-china, chipped at half-price, the fossils and jettisonings of a decayed life or more—once all these has-beens had been checked and chuckled over and out, and all the murmurings they brought to mind re-numbered, there were left in a hidden dark cranny, thick with dust, one or two small atoms of interest, that the travailer brought to loot.

'Did you know,' he feigningly said to Mr. Chinn, 'that you've been sitting on a gold-all-mine this time?'

'What are you too meaning to say?' said Mr. Chinn. 'Is it a picture that you've found, probably belongs to one of the older masters? Is it a gift I've inherited from my father? Probably a mystique whatever it is, a figurine, a forgery, a counterfeit.'

'More like a four-figure fat account for you in my esteem,' the dealer wheedled, 'less my own little personage, off-course, off-course. Mr. Chinn, I'll tell you your foretelling straight. I am a business-mammon, a trader to my cause, a profiteer without honesty in my own con-trade, I tell you this cunning-diddlingly. But even with my access to an excess cut and run, even with my over-takings, my under-handed handling of the overheads, even with allowances for all of this, still I can grandee you a profit, a bank-roll of dozens and dowsings of rods and purchases of divinings and fine things of fortune's weal beyond the dreams of Everest. You'll be worth waiting for in gold, Mr. Chinn, thousands of pounds and oncers and sumptuous precious stones.'

'But where,' said Mr. Chinn with mountain excitement, 'where is all this in-coming from?'

'Even with these brickbats and mantelpieces,' the man replied, piling in front of Mr. Chinn a mass of china oddments on end, 'you're beginning to hit the jampot. They'll fetch a bid or two down at Dotheboy's. But this,' he said, holding out his palm, the prize, 'this is the real winnow-

109

ing. This is what gives you the Mithras touch, the worth of a sun-king's ransacking, a king's ransom.'

He handed out to him three puny pennies, not a penance more, not even sovereigns. Mr. Chinn let out a groan, a grin, a sort of howl-and-ow laugh, a cry of penury. He hadn't been able to believe his lugs, and now he knew it was all a drachm. He had been cheapened, chatted into credit, and now he felt de-flattered, let down.

'Three coins aren't a fortune,' was all he could sigh.

'Look a little more longingly,' countered the coiner, 'look at them a gain.'

Mr. Chinn did as he was totalled, and began to see that this was endowed much more than coppers and rubbish. He began to recall a telling that Mr. Egg had told him before his leave-taking, a tale he had recoiled from at the time as another Egg-regius profession of false history.

'You see,' said the blandish-man, 'you beggar to see. It's a treasure to rave about, a dredging to rove around the world-width with, an unheard-of asian hoard, worth more than its troy-weighting in proven gilt.'

It was, o yes in dead certainty, what Mr. Egg had said, and had left behind him as part of the tip. He had heard Egg's-claimed tellings of these hidden ilians, this secret cash, these bent coppers found by Egg's-curvation, and belonging in their fiercest place to the goodness-grecian miser-known world of worrier Egg-a-memnon (he of Egg's-altered memory). This epicurean find (it could have been a most moving picture-show, an RKO-logical production of the centuries' flux), this fool's gold by rights belonged to Mr. Egg. But it was going towards making Mr. Chinn a far-enriching man, a walking heir to all the far-tumult that came down from the deuce from the harrowings of the unshent world—even though he had never before credited a word of his Egg's Troy denarii story.

A MARRIAGE IN
TWO MINDS

From being danged down in the dingy dumps, as he had been, Mr. Chinn slovenly found himself rolling in it. He was back on balance for the first time in his add-up life, as rich as Crassus, a triumpher, king of the Lido, splashing out at every importuning.

He found himself so hounded by friends he had never capitalised on in his life, and was at the deceiving end of all their in-fighting to be his host on the town, their quest, their rarest V.I.P. Now the fat cheques had come home to rustle in his nest-egg, he heard now anew oiled words from many wishing-wellers who had kept all off at harm's length during the leaning years.

There was one from his old-school palliative Albert, his old ally, an invasion to the welding together of a nuptial

111

friend, another class-mater from their mutual-hated former days. It was brawny Brian, the cricketer on the heath, who had boiled a madam over, a pert little pretty May Donne-Hood—also a brood of 2B, now a bride-to-be—and it was she who had picked her Brian, and was now about to lose herself her name, her voiled head, to sir, her née to his yes, so that together they would be a loving-cup: misfitter and misused Box.

Sitting in his place, Mr. Chinn could not hope looking upon their comedy, their union, their altar-ration, for his own. Though he had always kept himself inviolate, in clover, it set a-work in him deep buried burning sleeping longings to belong, tired homespun yearnings to be a pair, to beg a partner, old fool ties that he had never quite undone. And now May in her blooming whiteness, her bridle, her bosoming gown, and Brian well-groomed, with his tails held high, as they receded into the dissonance—the needing much appealing from the inner organs—they brought it all to the service once again. There was no naying it, no once again saying it: Brian and May made a very good match.

And as this struck, so it lit up in Mr. Chinn an old flame, and put the beginnings of an ardour into his head. It was an hour, several glasses later, that his wrecked ignition finally sparked. Brian by now was even the wordier the wistfuller for wear, and with many lewd loud rear-markings, doubtfully intended, he innuendoed and seduced Mr. Chinn to one of the bridesmaids, a broad small decayed young woman. Their eyes met across a rowdy groom. She was Maud, he was quickly unshored, overboard for her.

He lured her to the dancefloor, he kept her in his grope. He wooed if she cooed and they danced. She liked his balance, the state of his fine answers, his handsome features and fortune. He liked her chubby charms around his waste, her fingers on his treasured chest, touching his golden locks. She could span it all, as far as he was coerced, he would put her on a sound footing, so long as she kept him captive in her hands. She saw herself in endless shopping and changing, unloosed upon the high sprees. He saw himself in a quiet heaven, an arbour of you-and-me, she would be his savings at last. Pretty soon she was Harrod's-over-Heal's in love with him, and he was besieged, besought by her, besotted with her sotto vouchings, he so-low perfumes. He sighed to her, she swayed to him. And the conquest was that they were soon betrothed, bed-writhing, fiscal relations between them both, though they hurriedly knew one another at all.

Before the sun rose up, he found himself engorged, and it never once accursed to him how grossly he was faltering what his father had done before him, how far he was reappearing his parents' pattern of get-hitched-quick, on the spurt of the movement, of interring himself into a deranged marriage. Reader: he merited her; rider: she harried him.

A MATTER OF MONEY, OR WHOLLY DEADLOCK

Of course, he knew before belonging that this lusting would not last, this feeling in love at first suit. He knew it was almost all a terrible miss-take as soon as he reached the point of no right turn, no bacheloring away.

It had all happened in the flesh, in a hot flash, and he found himself walking up the knave of hearts, and assenting the great 'I will' (the I'll of caprice), without even a second's thought. He should have jolted her there and then, broken to her all his vice, left her in the lurch. But instead he took no stand at all, going through with the complete lack of emotions, like a numby-bum, like a zombie.

'Dearly bluffed,' the vigour intoned, 'we are tethered here to blather. If any man knows any cussed jaws or speech impediments, let him say his piece.' But no one put in their spoke.

'Wilt thou,' the priest pressed on, and he wilted. And she in turn intoned her yes-o-yes, her signal of distaff, of disdaining singleness, her willing coming to married blessed blush-ingness.

'Dost thou,' the pressing choired, 'dost thou agree to take it on the chin? To hug and to haggle from this day forewarned. For Worcester, for Perth; for Richmond, for Porlock; in Skegness and in Hull; till debtors depart.'

And he aggrieved to it all, heard himself mumbled before the lot of them, the conjugation, and signed himself away on the doting line. It all went with a hitch. There were rings on her fingers, bells on the nuptial ties, and cries of here comes the birdie as they stepped into stunned light to face the delighted camaraderie, the convivial fettering. All Mr. Chinn could hear, ego-ing inside himself, was the special threat, the victor's monstering last words still bristling on the air on the back of his necessity, 'Those whom the gods would junk together, they first put us under.'

It was then, only then, that he began to notice out of the cornea of his isolation where he was and everyone who was there—wife mother sister childer in-steps, frenzied relations, all the host of his second-guessings, old herded chums from the mad-nights of his youthless days, old faces from the forces. Albert was there as his accomplished best man-friend, the ring-leader of his old gangling times. Bruçe was there, dressed to kilt and laughing all the girls with his loathsome spiel. There was as well an unseen latecomer (a man with a brown mocking tash) who could have been a nobody, and might have been Mr. Egg in disguise and in disgust returned to hunt him down, but who left before he could be ticked off.

And then there was Maud, the latest in the chain of Chinns, enthralled by him, though he no longer thrilled at her. She was a dumpy blondish mossy-coloured moll, dull as ditchwater, a witch's daughter (as he only saw when he met his outlaws-to-be, a couple of swollen-headed swaggerers of the medium classes, middle-landed fogeys from the denser garden sub-herbs of surly and hull—a W.I. witch-sister with a sable-furred hissing sibyl-aunt, and a hag-ridden hubby whose only hobby was to get away on the inland avenues of waterways, to be a vulgar boatman, always asking where his craft was, Maud). He was stuck with her, withering here in the sticks. She would be a school-mister's missus, a misused wifey and a strain. She would bear his kiddings, hardly able to bear him at all. She would curse his biddings, and he hers. They would be at each other's heed not at all from the first. She stood at his sighing now, every clinch the fateful bride. He looked down upon her with something reproaching piety. He saw only too painfully plainly what he and she would be, the seducee and parasite, she the tempest-tressed acquirer of a reckless rustic swine—what he would always afterwards call after her, 'Carmen to the Gadarene, Maud'.

ET AL.

Then there was Albert, old alibi all-but, rising to his second fit, and offering to make some toast.

'La-di-dahs and jingo-men,' said Al loudly, rising to the accusation, looking a guest upon the dissembling shamble of piggy-wigs and froth-eared hatefuls. 'With your emissions I shall say a few well-chastened words.'

Mr. Chinn sat by his brood full of foreboding fruits. Already he could censor what was to come, already he had the wording guessed, held in his guilt-wrung eye, his guise.

Al looked about to speak, and cleared his threat. 'In the sight of goodness knows what,' he begabbled, 'and in the face of these here presents,'—he jested beyond the guests to the too many steam-irons in the foyer, the teeming cloths and the tedious services, the stintless rows of crested steel—'we are here to celibate, to elaborate the end of an era, the enduring of an earache by this mannikin to this wooing. We have this morning stewed and sat through a long serried moaning and a taxing ranked processional, a lining of hymns and hearses,'—one and Al thought back to the outline of black-marriers, of mirks and ribboned rolls, outside the kirk—'and now we are here to join enjoying in the what-mayhap, the future dismaying of this queen of the maybe on this high-priced prance amongst men—a fait-à-compliquer, a fête worse than death.

'I have known Mr. Chinn too long to resemble. We have been in-team-mates playing with each other, clash-mates clasped in each other's come-raids, in our armours in the campagne. I know him like the bark of my own hound, paining to be led in, licking nothing more than to be lapped up in a cuddle, in a coupling. I have known him to long to be enamoured, to be held in a loving embarrass, knotted, coming to know arms.

'Now he has himself Maud, this maid marrying herself to this rabid hound and all his merriment. Her I horridly know at all,' continued Al cholerically, 'but I can ensure that her parents will not be losing a ditto, but soon they will be gunning for the same. God, I fear for all this long poor tending. We must raise our eyes—unnerve the lass—above this doubled base reality, drink ourselves surly, drive onwards bumper to bumper, bless the wounded pride, and bless the grim. We must wish them both a lark, tell them that our hard-felt or gooey wishes go with them for a spree de coeur. But how long do we truly trially give them? Let us raise hour-glasses to the hapless pair, timed together in their defection. For I am banned bounding to say to you, my for-ending: I fear the wrench in marrying her; I fear thy Chinny clan.'

And so Al was said and done, and sat himself downcast in his uncheerfulness. But he was up and ready when the going was come—Mr. Chinn in his jeans and jacket, Maud in her trousseau, an ill-matched duel—throwing his petulance aside, his qualms in the air, with the rest of them, and wish-whooshing them a long fair while, all the blessed, fears standing in his eyes at their deep-hurting, and to the very last, the loss of them around the final turning, dear Albert Ross was hanging round his ancient's neck.

FIRST-CLASH
TRAVAILS

They drove themselves off—'Unjustly Martyred' sticky-lipped in red-lettering on the boot-end—and began their long fought nights of horny-moods and money-handling. They went off each other together almost immoderately, most heartily from the start.

Mr. Chinn wanted Maud to get away from her sorry silly-hole filly-stunted upbringing, wanted to get himself away from his school-hall incoming. He wanted her to see the pearls and doyens of culture, the sites and height and ABC's, the statures and pointings, the sheerest booty of the your-rapine tradition, and for himself to vista again the rebirth-replacement of his inert life.

He would take her to a hotel in Italy for their utterly idyllic idle-days, fly her to Florence for the days of her florescence, her away-kenning. When they arrived, Mr. Chinn raved and raptured on the balcony, rhapsodised in bel canto his craving for the via, the view. But Maud was not there, unaware, already bedded and snoring, ignoring his outpourings unaesthetically. Maud abroad was bored, and deadly.

On the days of their recreation that lay following, he took her about in a Fiat de Luxe. It was a lightning conducted tour, her ears splitting a-thunder at the endless din-formations, the gabble and gulping faction, the lifeless chill arty facts, which he never suck-ceased to thump into her between the ice-creams and the piazzas and the leaning towers of pasta. It was all too stuffy, she was so over-eating, so unschooled, in this ill-humid atmosphere of utmost fervour, that she could hardly stand any longer. She became increasingly incensedly bellicose at all the beautiful things he showered on her. At length, on her last legs, her damnation broke all at once, outburst him all over.

They were standing in the dusky Texan hills, on a peripeteia in Fuseli, when the dressing-down reversal came, a dusty ledge looking over the lodges and the villages, the age-old villas, and the distant vastness of the misty city billowing below them. 'Behold!' he said, holding her with one and drawing her with his other free-hand, showing her the plain, 'ecce duomo!'

'Stop!' she stormed. 'Not another step, not another word!' She stamped her foot, stammered her fury. 'I'm fed up,' she was carrying on, 'I've had enough. I never want to see another Grotto, another Ghetto, another Meek Angel or another Body Shawled. You can keep all your Vermicelli, all your Cannelloni, all your Phoenicians and all your Veneers. I want to see Valentino, Garbo, Brando. We spend all our precious largesse, all your precocious learning, we spend every day in the Uffizi from nine till five. I want to go to the pictures!'

Mr. Chinn was quiet, taken a step back at this torrent, this tirade. And then he said, 'With Firenze like this,' with a swipe of his arm across the scene, 'with Firenze like this, who needs cinemas?'

But in any case, the next day after, they packed and plugged up their lugs, their carriage, gave useful tips all round, and drove away. They left for the left bank in Paris, for the same little place that Mr. Chinn had a penchant for from his mixed-up salad days, his solo days, when first he sunk so low (ah, where are the snares of yes-to-yearning, the knaveries of Danton?).

And after their arrivederci, when they arrived, bowling down St.-Michelin in their little deux-chapeaux, their change of headgear, Mr. Chinn had a tiny minute's nostos, a twinge of neuralgia, a face-aching forsaken feeling for the place that had been his harm away from harmony, his habit.

He would take Maud to all the latest up-to-the-minuit film showings, all the home-mode movings of a new veiled vagueness, the made-up-and-combing starlights in shorts, with animated features, the scant and nervy, cheap and uneasy fore-running films with incompressible subtleties, the flicks and the rozzers in flesh-pot flea-pits. They stood in lines for the most reasoned icy Bergmanns, the True-faux, the Felony, the Bardo-latry, and spent hours waiting for Godard. Maud became invariably hot in the queues, itching in the heat, hating being in these alas sticky cities for so long at a stress.

'I've got to get out of here,' she mourned, she moaned, 'or out of my mind. I'm drying of thirst glass living. I need a cooling draught, a slow time by the lago, by the pool, the sea, to be aboard, be calmed, beaching, bathing, or both. If I don't get to some stretching of water soon, I'm going to go in Seine.'

'But,' said Mr. Chinn, wearily, bewildered, once bitter, twice shrewishly, 'with France like this,' and he indexed the autos and the bustle with his finger, the city's rough-cut and pricey night-life, 'with France like this, who needs any meres?'

And yet, yet again, he relented, landed them both back in a mellow marshland, in a dreamland of brooks and dykes, in a streamlined Ford he was loaned, a verdurous covered Lincoln, a flattened muddled mud-land midway between the solid soil and the sea. At first, it seemed that Maud was quenched, quite quieted, curled down. But then she began to develop her complaining, lay in bed in pain, in consternation, unable to move herself or her boils, blaming the seafood, the ageing mussels, the shellfish husbandry she was landed with. Her disloyal anus was her trouble, the sphincter of her discontent. Nearly demented, she demanded to be taken home to see her familiar doctor, who knew her as the family daughter, knew her insides out, a doddery G.P.I. who would give her the low relief, her cul the cooling ease and cure, the bum-balm, she needed.

Mr. Chinn stared the fate in the face, lost for words. In his mind he had already given up the guest-house, taken her backside to where she wanted, back to her mother's, even as he finally faintly muttered, not that it mattered, 'But with fens like these,' he pointed poignantly through the window to the wind-swept sweep of wetland, 'with fens like these, who needs enemas?'

A RUMOURED
FUN-ZONE

And so it wintered withering on, decay after decay, mood after waning moon, with many warning sighs, into their post-nuptial deep regression. They did not hit it off each other once from the first day of their harm-coming. Mr. Chinn, with his heigh-ho high hopes, his high-handed-down hopelessness, his bottomless belongings, was soon cast cursing down into his old unwell despair, the last hand-wringing rung of the ladder, last tread of the stairwell, by his lady-love, his load and mistress, weighed down by all her little ways. Maud, with her saddening sudden whims, her women's rites, was all thirst-raging, all frustration with him.

He had only ever wanted a safety match, an at-home all friendly, cuddly comfy candlelit companion, a panacea for all his illegalities, a dependant to his hearth's containment. She wanted to be expansive, unpensive, to spree, to spread her winnings, her free pinions, and to be out and about, outrageous and about with raggers and ravers, all the jolly ragtime. There was no keeping up with her purse, her pace, no staying up to her all hours, her late night finales.

And if she did not get her own away, or if he entertained the slightest demurest suspicion of another objective—such as, 'Could we not, my cooey dove, my duck, for once stop in tonight, and play a round of poker by the fireside? Or Weddington's Monogamy? Matches for bets. Before we make for bed'—or, some of the times, simply from her own exertions, her exhaustion, she would take to her realm, to her boudoir, unbidden, in a sulk or an ill-fit or sickening from his or her complaints, his lack of compliance. Then there was a thick horrid frostiness between them, a tough rigid utmost fury. She would be the preening madonna, giving herself great arias, putting herself under a heavy sedateness, from which Mr. Chinn could only freeze and free her by giving in to all her little weak needs, her traits, her cupidities, with endless trays of cups of teas, and buttering her up with rounds of toast he brought her, the crustiness cut off. Thus fussing, he would bring her round, and the whole sick cycle start again.

He had thought he had heard that it would all be a floral frolic, unnumbered days of winding paths and primroses, that the romance's pleasure was in the marital home, the hearth's ease, where together they could sit out their days, hubby ever laughter. He had not reckoned or sealed it properly with Maud. The trough of the matter, of the whole murderous mad matrimoaning Maud-recital, was that on the subject of women Mr. Chinn quickly knew knout. He should never have got evolved.

Maud soon took the upper hand, took in an upright grand into their little lounge against his wall, lunged herself at it like a conceited pleonast, a Clamorous Shoeman banging on

125

to the last. Under the veil of tears of their endless rowdying in all those dark ages, she would bash him out of doors, or bash out hymns on the old hosannah—there was a touch of methodism in her malice—so that their angering and ergo-ing would end in 'Unwed Christian solitaries, watching out for more!' until a kind of pain-fought silence, a lost accord, was restored. He knew that she would be the running of him when she bought herself a furtive coat in their first pelting winter (a real Chinn-chiller), a little sparky spurts-car on the spot, and would not let him get his hands on her waste, tantara-ing and drumming out her crotchety turns on the piano until he re-lent her his last penny, and held out to her his piece.

In time, in sixty-eight time it must have been, she joined the women's liberace movement (a clean-cut case of pianist envy, in Mr. Chinn's dim view of things). Then there was no halting her at all, no question of her being Maud or marred by his inventions, no chance of muddling maudlin through to a better end. He could not be a pig-male to all her lies and doing little, her gall and tears. She told him to think deeply dopily about the statues of women in our society, and to stop putting her in a purdah-style, to give her her libido, the basic kneads of ladies: free Guinness, a private nincompoop to handle, and an aroma they could call their own. He could see how she sulphured, how behind every great cretin of man their lies a gored woman. But he was daft and bland to every demeaning demand she made for him to change his ways and wherefores: doomed if he did, doomed if he dissident.

126

DIVORCE OF CIRCUMSTANCES

It came to a pretty pass, to a parting of the ways and means
between them. It was, as they say, as Albert had said it
would, willy-nil be, inevitable, unenviable, a never-to-
belong saying of so-long. Theirs was a soon off, shoddy gone,
short-loved marriage, a hot-headed mirage quick in the
deserting. It was a life-hurt relationship, where they only
wanted each other's holdings—her arms, his shares—for
their own, no goods at all.

Maud's invalidities, her indelicacies, were famed and
farmed out from the first, the franker language of all the local
loquacious hot-gossipers, the common tongue-waggers of
the hostelries, remarked in all the public barbs and easy-
speaking insolences. It was all over, bar the shouting, over
the school, the whole town over, the surrounding laundries,

127

the bars, the shopping-centre, even before they had set all down. They were always washing their dirty linkings in public, and Maud was always soiling herself, hanging her repute on the line. She had had her hard-working wriggling way through with most of the other misters, unbent some of the stuffy, stiff members of the staff-room, and begun to take most of the sturdiest first fifteen-year olds, the scrum of the earth, in hand, in her stride, passing over the studious, the eschewed, and the flies of the swats. She had started on most of the lower forms of sex with the best of the sixth, made her first forays into the woods with the townsfolk—the commerce of chambers, the old boys, and the stray men of affairs who used to gather under the town-hall clerk—and made herself free with the farmers' hands and the out-and-out liars for mills around, the pokers and the gamesome-peekers alike.

Even on their horned-moon crescent of a tidal wave together, she had locked Mr. Chinn in the Louvre and gone off to a tiny park to perk up a young heartsore Sorbonnard, one Pierre, a stone's-throw from the Neutered Dome, where Maud by the water's sedge of the River Sin had had her island fling. The truth was that from the beginning she was a whorey flying propositioner, a bitter tart from Eve's original apple, a meddler. She was no bedder than she should be, a little hotted-up swish swedish model could not have done more or worse than she did, driving her vulva at a cruising speed of over ninety males a year, crash after crush, puncture after punter.

And what's a constant instant peccant source for every gossip is source for every slander. Mr. Chinn too, driven to it, was no different, no more diffident than her. His only probable blame was that Maud had got to all the best boys, the best buys and biceps in the tup-shop—the long-haired destined runners, the disco-party throwers and the breast-strokers—before him, behind his backwardness, and he was

128

left with the base mean buggings, the crawlers, the cheap spoiled goody-goodies and the pretty willing anybodies.

All this, in no time, at night-time, unerringly eerily recalled up the recoiled-from Mr. Egg to the scene of the crammer (the first time since their call-up). He came, the wicked whisky-pissed pixie, Mr. Chinn's old poxy proxy, his evil genie, bent double, out of his shell-hole, his winter watering-palace, his spartan spa-town or low-cost coastal resource, when he heard the call, the coil that Mr. Chinn was in. He could not be kept at St. Evil's Bay, at Chiltern-arm's length, at any queer's cove, in any silly white man's Egg's-isle, any bally high and dry, for ever, without coming out of his Elba, returning to his old stampeding-ground, his chump, his camp-follower.

Having Mr. Egg around, run aground, only made things worse, whizzed them to their disillusion, sundered them sooner rather than loitering. Maud had no interest left in Mr. Chinn, once the earliest earnings were gone, all the balance, the equal librae all run through. She found him temptable and conned when he was drunken, and borrowing a shell when he was sombre. She hated what lethal she saw of Mr. Egg. And as for Mr. Chinn, there were all kindlings, all little things of manners in Maud, that incensed him, small mannerisms he had always minded in his mother's superior ways—as well as her celerity in sin, her little insincerities, the stupid insipid way she drank from her cups, all her vast hideousness in the face of meals to be mouthed, the way she was at table, hatable, finicky, fanatical, the way she held herself, her culturedness and cutlery, naif and faux.

Everything came to the head, and the boss hit the roof, when with Mr. Egg on his worst mis-behalf, carrying himself on and on like the loudest least suited full-mouthed tiddly boor, and Mr. Chinn a swell, they led the winning lads of the hick-hacking hicupping hokey-jokey team on an up-aloft-ing hike-as-a-kite-bag hickory-victory-mock mickey-taking myth-anarchic midnight rowdy proud parade, a carousing and careering carry-on in an abandoned out-of-bounders corner of the grounds. It was a swell elaboration out of all sorts. There was much whooping and loud-hailing and joshing of Keith (the cap-retainer of the tumult), a night of guying abundance which reached its crime-acts when Keith was disembodied of his clobbering, and his pallid form ran shirtless and shortless, graceless in the wet grass, in his all no togs to gather, under the loon-light, and out into the lane, screaming for a halt, for a hide, running for cover. They were fine rabbles, revelling luminaries, these lordless lads, until the coming of the pleas, the air-wresting overseers, the holders-up of lore and horrider. Then suddenly the fine fun was at a bidden end, and Mr. Chinn saw the cursed cost of it all, the damages he was immersed in, and that his only outweighing downwards redress, his soul's Egg's-it, lay in the way of all flashers, all fell demons, in his devilry with the pack. He would have to pay with his cards all right.

After every legless rapture is the rupture, the catch. Mr. Chinn, the morning after, went ducking and aching into the head's low room, a note of resignation in his voice, his hand. It was a way past his chucking-out time in any cause, and he would go quittingly, waiving the pay for a new beg-innings, a new life turned over. He got the handshakes he deserved, and no thanks, nothing, for all his years of severance. He would not make a farouche stir of it all. He would make a fresh start, would vanish Mr. Egg to an utter limb, o to an out-and-outer dungeness, a nether-nether land beyond the poles. He would move heaven and oeuf to be rid of him.

And then when he got back to the house, released, he found yet another note, left with the keys on the piano-stool, a crabbed scribble in Maud's farewell hand. It told him she had run off with the hidden cash-box and an indian runner, a bum-boy currier, name of Singh, a reedy warbler in the choir who had been her latest poppet, her puppet, no strings

130

attached (Mr. Chinn's legs for a sickened moment turned to green jealousy as he read on), and she would not be back, come what dismay. 'I can,' she wrought, he read, 'no longer understand, my drear, a life, or lie, with you.'

It was all over, a lover between them, a parroting of the why and wherefores. He stood in the half-way place, in the hallway, neither won nor another, and realised his loss again, his solace-tidings, his all lowness. He had reached adultery, his lot in life, no longer a kidding of himself for complacency, a softy-certain. Mr. Egg was dispatched, Maud had made off, and now Mr. Chinn would go all so, all solo out into the migrating great unowned.

MR.
CHINN
FREE

COLLAPSE, O (PART OF AN ODDITY)

Mr. Chinn had always enjoyed with relish the unheard-of organs of priests and fools, the churned-out remainders of their journal-houses, the offal offerings of their whining presses. It was a habit pickled up from his American days, the relish. He liked thick gibberish stew, the rodent's digest, tit-bits, paunch, the ill-assorted news. He always took the tablet after meals, the chewy tonic.

Whether dunked or lewd or slobbered up, or just as nominal, he always thought of himself first off as an ordinary old-Henry sort of philo, liking anyone else, any tomfool or dickhead, with a nominal sort of no-odd job, a Sid'n'Terry occupation—no respecter of parsons, no man of the purple, a chap off the old bloke, Mr. Avarice, silt of the earth, l'homme croyant sans sueur (a gullible fellow-traveller, nose wet).

135

But now, standing stunned in the hall of a doubter, all of a dither, he couldn't credo or read a thing, sorely saw sunkenly that all this had never been, this reverie-man, this man of the straight. He had lost his gift of the job, his happy tight, he couldn't eat or hate or hit a thing, he couldn't take another half-berk nosh or nonsense, that wouldn't stick in his cranium. He had had a bellyful, a below-foul taste of bitter times to come. He was fed up, almost felled, fierce-some, truly veracious.

Here he was, depreciating his forte, whatever it was, approaching his forties, not roaring to go but cut adrift, a would-be raftless, a rift within the whole lot, going down the whole bang shoot, a cutter drifting, a cussed awry, tears coursing down on the day the cheek of it that ever he should have reached his disdained, destined bourn, his berth: the foetal mistake, a stunted man from the very first reelings, a freckle of nativity, a moonstruck oddity, a monstrosity from the staggering start.

This all a long, long time has been the tail-end of the life of a man who lives his slice over a pannikin. Goes from day to day on the thin-skidding thin ice into whose far-easing waters he at any moment might fall and drown. Lives in his slippers slithering at the edge of a pressure-piece, the heart-quake, giving everything away—his positions, his heart's contents, his last confidences—beneath him. Now he is still standing for a moment, perilous, powerless, paralysed, we can measure the wit and breath of him, the last lingerings, the affronted and sighing enervation. Before the demorali-sation, the de-malicious work begins. He is on his last legs now, the last new storey before it all comes trembling down, last age of his churning, his swilling bitter-pill grimace.

Prepare to meet thy pantomimic doom. Prepare for the final certainty, the concluding fact in this free-wheeler, the denudement, the apologue, a pause, followed by slow claps.

THE ASININE ARTICLES

What did he do, first off, what diddy-doo? He did not yell or yield, or scram outside out loud. He did not go down on his needs, and pry, not to beg inwith his own hame stayed. Nor did he hold himself sternly stockily, no bally-hoo, to savour the stealings and borrowings of his Trojan fortune. He did not whistle (Toby or not Toby) la-la-lee, or hum a reveller's bolero.

Fast thing he does is run up the uphill and peers, the old appeal and lair of his chill-hoodwinked days, scene of his oldest dreads and rousings, where he first felt himself betrayed and erased, the am-between place of his am-baffling life. Stares headlong ahead of him, gazing into vacated spaces.

What is he lurking for? The self-same as ever, the sem-

137

blance of an I-density he can call his onus, which he can only find by feigning or fondling himself in another, or in all the nothings, the noughts and orts and odds and end-bits, the baubles, the borrowings, the trashery, the truncated cut-offs, that others leave behind—a re-assembly of himself from all the mass of the mess, in all the abiding filth and heap and carrion (these three, but the cruddiest of these is carrion), in which he might find an inner piece, a soiled solid base for himself.

There was a second-hand colourless shirt; a fun-for-all pile of old comics; a golden locket of dye-dote's hair; a fading cutting from his own first stage; a lost-life album of happy family snap-cards; an expunged bag; an oak-famed landscape with broken glass; a yellowing tome of Browning from his schooldays; a star-gawpers' charter; a money-pocket falling to purses; a burrowed adventure-book to which he had never returned; a present ribbon from Christmas past; a tousled banquet from their peach-nicking days; the marooned symbolical cord of his plaited dressing-gown; an unread damnable rational book; a postcard with mushy love from mydearie; a grade-book to the many steps of St. Palsy's; a burned-all bundle of his school reputes; a measure of his hexameter results; his first face in his first passe-partout; a scrap of scarf from his collage; a once-worn burst bib and tuxedo; a forgotten sea-veneer of brittle rock; a sheaf of assessors written in a bind; two scrupled versions from his love-piety; a deducted copy of B. Campbell's monogram; a row of precocious meddlings; an at-a-loss of the world; an ostracised egg; an uncrushed doler's cheque; a pawed graphic homage to two men, tipsy-pervy; a lads' register of whipping; a botched pot, never sold; a visitation to a widowing, 'Mr. and Mrs. Dunder-Head require the pledge, R.I.P.'; the dried-up flutters of Maud's bookie; the broken iced heart from the wedding-carcass; a sum of lost exchange in liars and franknesses; some few score loose cheats of Maud's musings; and

138

deep piles of her take-care-pet tacked away French lovers' letters, and other manys, done up in alas-sticky bonds. And, in editions, many old unfired and unfair magazines and pyres of moccasins he had never quite thrown out of, never let slip or quit himself of, or kindled with the spirits in the flames. And other such atoms of uninterest. These unfuelled things were all that remained to him of him.

These are the selves you lonely find in drawers, in uncertain cases, on shelves, amongst the unbelongings, the loose leafings, the mistakings and the bleaker black. This was all that Mr. Chinn could lay his hands on in the infernal hidden regresses of his self-possessions, in all the piles of ironing and filings, amidst the undefiled and underwear— these thirty-nine re-trashing steps, the check-stubs, the dirty unknown articles of his be-life. Nothing to hang together, nothing he could call his sewn-up selfhood, his owned-up head-covering to keep off the impending, the impeding brainstorm.

A SEMI-MENTAL
JOURNEY

S uddenly couldn't stand it still any more, couldn't draw breadth in these confines, in all this clutch. Came clattering down the stark stairway, and had to get out into the opiate air, into outer breathe-easy wild open spaces, to full-fill his lungs, to face the blows.

He stood in a field feeling the unhindered weight of the lift of the sky above him, bearing down on his should-be, and the brown clouds and the clods below him, the blades of grass whetted beneath his feet, standing on his naïve soil. He was looking for a land-escape he could call his seed-sown own, a glorious pasture with a few game chicks, a little rusty bridge now and then, the odd folly—somewhere he could be a fissure, could cull-divert his jordan, could meditate on what Maud did, contemplating his gorgon, and ponder with complete anger the complicit fool he had been, how he had fallen for her looks loins and sincerity, down by the old maelstrom. He found no piece of land not mined in this heart-acred patch, nowhere free of the muddied murderous thoughts that rose elementally in his ill-mannered soul, his ill-manured soil, the desire to be acquitted of her, the brute brooding wish to see the whole issue buried, to see the blunder-red hips and berries on the tree (or, as Jock the Strapper was asked by his son, 'Why did you do in the whores, daddy?').

He had to get even a further distance away, to put the millstones between them both. Went to all the extremities of this our outer isle, both north and south, away from all the knavery, trying to find the place of mind for his roomy nations.

Went to the west land first, to the land of his father's and mirthsome holidays, to Trepanning in Corn-laws, and Lland-send and Jonah-grates in the bellies, in the valleys, of squel-ched Wales. He stood on heaths, on cliffs, on weathered heights, and considered his position, thought often of making himself a jumper, a palaver, before the cold prescrip-tion and the rotten weather set in, smashing his numskull out on the gulleys of the ravines of the rocks below him—food for the fettered and the finicky kinds.

In such distraughts, in fade-away districts where one could despair without trace, a man will cadge at the least straws, at any stray surety in the wind. It was in such and such a station that Mr. Chinn heard word that his old friend for himself was back from a base abroad. This was it, the story that Bruce the Campbell was back—back from an outback deserted anti-posting, selling Austen and Morris to the Easter Isle aliens and the whizzkids of Oz, back with a banger of his own, to an easy chair and a cushioned position, a long steady reign, in the pouring poor rigid far-city of Gaberdine.

And so Mr. Chinn plucked up his carriage, his mac, his long johns and small remaining silver, his meek and oily skills, and travelled over sleepy terrains, inviting himself for the long a-wetted winter months, for a cold spell of the Hibernian nation. Bruce's price for bread and abode was his usual constant inconsistence on having a highland skittish fling. With this, and what was forked and cast out every month on account of old Maud's alimony knack, in a quick while of misfortune Mr. Chinn was skint and barely alive. He sought any sort of job, any ordinary Nairn to Fife employment, but they only wanted deciduous workers whose leave fell off with the onset of autumn. There was nothing doing to be done. With his money all outgoing and gone, and his luck and his coat worn thin, he looked for a comforter in a warm Scotch brothel, scraggy ends of limbs and leggings to chew on, but little chance of any real meat to bring back feeling to his lingering ends, or to his toe-tips, numinous with cold from his shivering-leaked boots.

Bruce scoffed at his discomfiture with the old stale stylishness of his codded days. He tried to melt him down with malts, with the twelve-year distillations of his long experiences. When this was bootless, he thaw-fully loaned him a well-knit scarf. Mr. Chinn thanked him warmly, but his cold shoulders did not mend, his stiff neck bend. 'The fault, dear Bruce,' he said, 'is not in our scarves, but in our cellular underthings'—though he knew well-fuelled that it was lowlier still, that it lay deep in his soles, where the damp nation entered in, where his ill, sodden, unshoddy lack of grounding was to be found, in a part beyond where any cobbler can a state of pleasuredom decree.

LOW-DOWN PRIED, A HAS-BEEN HANDED DOWN

He found himself high and not dry, needing an embrace he would never get from Bruce, and not knowing which way who he could turn into. He could not face a marmoreal Albert, having ignored with Maud his stern guile-warning. His relations with Sis had almost ceased since her defection to her bossy posh husband, his brother-in-lieu. And Mummy was dead, yes, dead as a toenail, cut off in her prim and propped-up bunk alone—he had coldly kissed her ashen cheek in the casket, and sung 'Goodbye with me' as they had interred her, sent her to oven, done to an urn.

Faced with such a het-up head and heart-ague, unable to choose, hardly able to hobble in his shoes or choose, he went back up to Lone-down town, his centre of depravity, his ill abode, the place where he could most diseasedly think

143

without trace. He had not been there ten minutes in a dozen years, when the dizzying tiers of the new immense-city, the dismal dismantled tracts of the old poor-city, struck him thumbs down. Buildings more and more packed standing together, grand tenements and terminals now in dark lines, terrorist housing, hair-raising blocks of fact, waste indigent hassling estates all bunched together shack by gaol—this was what his ill looking's cross eye saw, standing out, the shitty life.

To cap it all, first poison that he chanced to meet—as lack would have it, first throw of the die—who should he bum into round the very first thirst-inducing bender, but his old Nick namesake, with 'Drink With Me' written on his lapel, Mr. Egg, chief mischief-maker, leader of mishaps as a rule? He thought he had sent him off for no good after the hockey-team rocketing, and that in the city's crudded unamity he would be at ease to lose trick of him, to keep his double bluffed. But here he was, as large as lucifer, and twice as harmful.

After a couple of well-earned pints together, after the public beers were bolted, Mr. Chinn was desperate for a piss-alley (go worst, young man), and in no time out of his mind at all he was down in the self-abasements, lost in the lavvy-rinse, just like all the old timers, all the old lags, enduring all the fun of the fairies—and already after a couple of well-brawned punters together over in the corner of the haunt. Whether Mr. Egg had followed, he was too fuddled, too tiddly and winking to notice.

Such elicited pleasures made him feel in touch again, brought him back to his since, with warm-blooded bonding in his reach, standing in close pricks' amity, hands across the lack of emotion. It had been a longing time now he had been pretty well a-sensual, after the first mad mauled days with Maud (what they hadn't done in those first free long bed-of-rousing days, where they hadn't hidden been, o which wishes

144

hadn't been sired and re-sired, which dishes from a menu, which fresh pages turned from a manual, o come, o come). He had had his truant taste of it, and now his all-embarrassing holophiliac hetero-generosity, his omni-venery, required a public outlet, whoever outlawed or outlandish.

In this, the enter-world he came to, his fellow fooled befoulers, all of them sully-willies to a man, were all of them equivocal, on an eager footing, the lowest commonest denim-doting contaminators, all of them thinking others nastier, nuttier or sadder might have been than they. In this dim hypocrisy, when a forthcoming change-like angelic boy seemed to reproach him (there'll always be a bland blonde, he enchanted to himself, and bland blondes shall be free), he found himself turning to his first compulsion, and saying, 'We are making our souls of ourselves'. And to his other chump before him, 'I'll leave you for later,' and walked away, out into the flesh-breeding air, a moment to respire, a moment of respite—a failed escapade temptation, knowing that whatever he might have done now to secede, he would pry, pry, pry again.

THE SABBATH-DAY NIGHT'S VARIETIES OF RELIGIOUS EXPIRATION

It had been like a flashing moment's conversion, this conversation, a damned-if-he'll-ask-us experience. Why was he killing time again with all the pricks? He felt a little for-shaken on his feet, and sank sanctimoniously moaning to his pins and knees, in the attitude of a prior.

When he came back he was on the street and neurotic outside St. Poor-Low's, sick of the repulsion, outside Vast-Monster Babble, the Catholic-Drawl. What struck in his mind's eye were these and thines and those block-letter notices, 'Christ Sighed For Your Dins', 'I Am the Why, the Wrath, the Aloof, and No-One Cometh Any Farther, But Barmy', 'Jesus Sieves'. He stayed staring stary-eyed, it was an answer to his pryings. He could hardly leave himself be, believe himself one of the slaved, one of the chastened furies.

Was this the deification he had always been dustbinned for, the privy-dance? God, he divined, had moved in queerer mazes before now, more mass-hysterical, more mistake-all. And so he felt no hazard in holding hands in a beatitude of prurience, in the imposture of a praying mannerist, and saying outlying, 'O Lord, Lord, I bluff. Help though my bumble-fluff. O keep me clinging and puerile. O Hallowed-loofah! O Holy-Roller! O How-de-doo!' (with a full-volume over-herded corral and the Hallelujah Orchestra, converted en masse by St. John Barcarole, the Water-Musical Handle-man).

This was the begetting of his bigotries, his turning over of new beliefs, his search for a faith in the crowd. He sat at the back during the hollow commotion, listening to the intoning of the lethargy, and watching the priestly digitator handle the goods, just like one of the impostors, one of the master-baker's dozen, saying, 'Take, heat, this is my fodder, use your loaf, lose your life. Abraham-cadaverous-ham, holus-bolus, hic-hac-hoc, turn this cracker into a cock.' And in the glow of the caudle-lit lamb-plight, he saw the conjuration go forward to receive the supreme saccharine device, the sweetbreads and the buried elder-wine—triune in the prophecy of your own tomb, suscitation guaranteed, or return after three days. But he could not take it, could not join or jaunt in their professions, any more than he could have cannon-ballsed up the corpus of a zealous mission-troupe in a zulu's pot, or eaten out the steak-red heart of a victim's victuals in another inca-nation.

It was no better in the See of Ely than amongst the friar-work display of the candle-holding Roman Catherine-Wheels, or the spinsters and the Cathar sisters in the abysses. And it was infinitely worse shopping around amongst the Press-Buttons, or the Melodists, or the Unabashed, or the Wee Free Kinks of Albania; or amongst the faking cults of the Seventh-Day Adventurists, the Church of the Saturday

Saints (he always shut his bolt against the Mormon invasion or the knocking of Jove's What-Nots), the Shakers, the Quakers, with their Christian silence, or the god-fleering last trumpeters of the Sally-Alley Pally-Army, the sobriety of friends (little surety they had ever shown him when his nadir was at its greatest, the lowest of these their fellow-breathers).

Or when he cast his church-search wider, pulling rabbis out of huts, or hammering on the doors of musclemen to categorize them in their schisms, he still found nothing that would stick in his credo. He daily dutifully examined the state of the Mecca, considering whether to put his saving into guilts or futures, reading all he could of the Tao-Jain averages, the misty schemes of the great eastern prophets. He listened to what confusion said, but only found himself further impaled on the horns of a dalai-lama, tossed and torn on the high unimaginable demands of every route he came to, and the low demeaning magic of its rites. He said, 'I kneel to make both ends meet in me, to make them mate, match and merge when they do not otherwise join at all. This is the only purpose of my brash hoped-for mitring, my mortification and tenet-seeking. But there is no fitting, no meeting, high deals and low things are still as severed apart. Stoics and saints may baulk my brains, and gnomes may ever haunt me. But the one wondrous won-in-one, the altogether, will never come.'

The more he heard of all their unhumble pieties, the more he heard inside himself—inside the whims, the heartache and the fear—just one stale smelly vice, saying, 'You are what you are, you-are-what-you-are, yah-hah wot yah-hah, yahoo-yah, yahoo-yah!' And within the clamour and the counter-clamours of all their brays and summons, their cant and canticles and well-conned texts, this single unsavoury saying was all he heard, until he could hardly drawl breath or semi-breaths at all.

In such an exhausted, dire fragmenting of himself, he found himself gasping in a gospellers' hall, forcing his rasping throat, his pent-up intercostals to join in the joy-din of their go-go-gossiping, their pray-singing the loudest laud, unsingly unstintingly singing along with all their throngs. And then, in the midst, the impossible apostolic success came down upon him, the dreadful gift of fire-tongs ('Just what I've always been warned of'), the pretty awesome penny-costing presence. With all the others, all the chanters shouting out forgetfulness for all their shindies, Mr. Chinn lost himself in singing with a forked-riven tongue, in all slangs, all languages, all lingos and none, all argots and naught, all unprinted pidgins pied, all idiotic syncretic idiosyncratic idioms. He spoke gibbering anguish at his whit-sunday wits' end. And went running into the streets to gabble up the gooned news to all the people, that the global goblin was dead and gone, god in his ghostly goodness in his ghastly goredness had come indeed.

TO THE
DARK HOUSE

They found him in a bad way, in a state of natter, on the by-pass, grabbing passers-by and garbling out his gospel at them, sniggering snatches of hymns and heresies, and serving them up the hot-spittle of his salivation in a babble of holy writ. 'I am what I am,' was his louder claim. 'I am good golly. I am the promised Monsieur, I am Jazzy Christy, the master-minstrel of the tree-o. This is Symbo, this is Bones. I am Neapolitan Torn-Apart, the ruling-pin, the lyncher of the whole known wold. I am Duo, I am Dio-Niceness. O folly me!' Mr. Chinn was a minister, a monster, a man-eater, a minotaur—mythic in his madness.

He was taken to a house-pitiful, to a quiet ward. They said, 'You need to have your headaches amended.' They said,

'We're going to take your pantings down.' They said, 'Don't weary, this will only halt for a second.'

Karma now. They transfixed him to the Department of Cynical Psephology, to see what was happening in his poll, to give him electoral shocks. He came to the room marked 'Circuitry', 'For goodness' sake, elope, all yahoos sent to here,' over the sorry door. There he saw the head-man, the shrieker, who asked him quietly sort of ouchy questions, quizzed him on his delight as a father, on his desires for murther, on his sublime sybilline relatings—all the fey-retelling stories he had known in which the witch and the bogie were distraught, and the preen-sis and the poor-runt marionetted, and leaped happily over rafters.

He told them some of all he remembered about his very little self, and what they already knew, what was already old tittle-tat to them. But he told them none of his sacreds. Not a jotting, he did not give away a clue, a nail-clipping in his coffin, in his confidences, not a wisp or whisper about the dark room, the little deed-end darkened room, and Dad at the dead of night, and under the cover of darkness, under the covers, and the fond hand—and where it led, all the depths of innermost darkness it had plumbed, man and boy, ever farther, ever more sunken, down all those years and layers between. Of this, the little nursery nest, where his nasty, his schism, his necessity, his itch, was first hatched out, where he first went cuckoo, not a word, not for the world, not for the worthiest wiliest in-terror-begetter, neither medicine-man nor priest nor good friends' hearing. He would take it, it would take him, to his grief, to the very dead centre of his graveness.

He did let slip the dog-eared lie (perhaps they had put him under some sort of hob-nobbying noseying, some hypnotic oaf) concerning his acquittance with Mr. Egg. And this un-Egg-spectred added problem caused them much in the way of speculation, much peculiar interest in just who was this addled Egg, this Egg-strawed-and-airy man, whose coy-Egg's-constancy with Mr. Chinn was doing so much to try and stray their patient, setting him up this bad Egg-symbol.

The more they pressed, the nearer the murk, the less black ground he gave, thinking in his own quixotic sand-blind way, his own quacked mirage, that he could salve himself thus, find his own solution, his own do-sip ointment. And their kink-illusion, their agnosis was that he was in low spirits, chthonically ill. 'You must pill your sex up,' was their prescription, 'take that, and that, and that.' 'Canoe thyself,' said the pseud-alienist, 'peddle your own knowledge.'

But he shrank from their injunctions, as he had shrieked at their injections. He knew himself unwell enough without their raids on his memory. He knew that he was always up and down like a ho-ho, everything black and white in rapid unchecked succession. Certifiably he was a manichean depressive, droopy and restive, if they wanted a tome for him, a locus for him in their spy-chicanery, their sick-allergy. He was never settled for a minute, saddled with it for a lifetime. He would try to be more real elastic, more reflexive, for hours at a stretch, though he was not constricted so to be. But first he had to find a way away from the padded locked-up brain-cells, the bleak imaginings, the black machinations, of these watch doctors, of this ju-ju salem.

He did it one day, much to his own sore prize, in the face of his own suppressions, by traducing a nervous nurse to worm into his bedding (a Norse nurse, a scold, who frigidly hailed and held him from above her antic circle, the lend of her lap) sedating her with the potency of his own pills and potions. He left her snoring, and walked out of the ward, robed in her own robbed skirt and under-form, her own stolen nylons and buckled belt, scuttled through the hop-skip and out into the fresh agile air, seeking liberty, seeking levity—finally turning on his new high healer's heels, and as farced as he was, he ran like mad.

A POOR TRAIT OF THE AUTISTIC

Dressed in the drag of the drugged she-dragon, Mr. Chinn's first thought was in no wise to redress himself, to re-cover his man-afield apparelled errancies, his oldest male-addiction. No, he liked his flee-male swagger, his new being in disguise, in this lass's aspect, caught up in her inter-garments. He had always nursed a secret impassioned ambition to be his wayward sister, and now he could be at least a miss-shaped vision of herself in the me-error on his shelf. He could change his leper's spots and all that he saw for a new skin, a new scan, a new-her-sis outlook.

What was in his made-up mind for the immoderate moment was to find himself somewhere an income for a table, a hard-backed share, an in-desk crippled pose, any

153

sloped desk where he might sit and set down his condition on paper. He wanted to get between clean sheets, not for a sleep for a change, not because he was feeling purely any more—his godhead splitting, spluttering out the new confidence, the second conning. He was through with that, through with seeking and sinning through thick and thin. Perhaps it was his stolen gift of the garb that incited him, made it possible by bringing to his service a pale incestuous doubling: two longings making one write.

He would try to regorge his hindermost thoughts in deftless prose, in sermony words, in a pure cursive contemplative style, the talking riddle-hums of his drum-attic idiomtom-tomes. He would sort fit words to point out the bleakest face of wo-ho-ho, to illuminate his lettering, dot and dash off the crass I's and teasings, and so leave behind him at the very last a few well-discomposed lost words, an enunciation of his limp-ending deep artfulness, a row of grave stanzas (in emporium) each in his own pun-name, a last wail and terse torment (leaving nothing to the imagination). And so scrawl towards death, on his handwritings and nuances, down on his a-plus-fours, a fool's cap pulled formly over his browsings, chewing on the end of his be-rôle, his bequest, his quest to be.

He had tried everything else he could thank to find an I.D. in his head, in his possessions, to look amongst the objectives of his life, and foundered on nothing. Had tried travel pursuits, and journeyed to the folk-owners of the hearth, and feigned no confraternity there. He had descended into the end-trails of the city's sewer-effluent so-perverse life, with small suck-cess. He had tried saving faith, and had failed dismissively. Had tried for the cure of his soul, with meddle-sin, drunk-will-easers and doctrine, but this had only made things worse (and maddened one thin nurse). What else could he do? Sixth try of the dice, last losing but one. What other line could he take? Trite writing.

He had hoped he might start a new word order, an entire new glamour, a whole new mana of sparkling, of in-spiralling speaking, with its own new shiny texts and new lex to stand on, a new aura in the hear-story of the unversed. It was a noble prize he aimed for, even though being famished was the spur of the moment. He knew poets were pawned and not paid, but even so it was a life and not a living he needed to make. With this garret and styx ensuring policy in his mind, which was the choice he was stark with, he began to set all down. But as soon as he stuttered, he could feel it all fail and fade, the craft ebbing. The mute was silent, the well run dry, not an inkling in his head. He had only to face his own crabbed hand scrabbling sideways along the blank, his own wistful papers in piles of heaplessness, all his dejected members, his limited ideas, unlimned, crippled, scrapped, wasted, flawed.

CRI
DE CURSE

He would gladly lavishly have written an epoch-making poem, a golden treachery in five tracts, a triple-decorated waffle, a mad-jesting work of orthography, *The Laugh and Romance of Me-Star Charlatan Chan* (best-seller of the excerpted), a divinitive medic-evil history of Chinn-glands. Grand visions and revisions drew him on. Quires of uncials sent him to his desk. Publishers all said, 'We will call you Anon.' But when it came to it, he was reduced to a few sellables, to cheap thrillers, books in phrases of pooh-dolls or house-plants or horseplay or trivials across the say-hurrah, or up the amazement, or down the know-all. To quick handy books titillated *1000 Things You Always Wanted Too, No?*, and gift books of recipients for the coffer-table, hint-books for making ready savings and

156

snack-bites ('many are cold, but a few have cheese on').

Out of it all, only one complete conceited dogma remained, unconcerned to the flimsies, to the fire, in another author of failure. And even that one had a tear on it, the writing blubbed by warping. It was a signalled sheet of paper, sign of his hard times, left in the carriage upon his harried departure, his last debauch. It was a farewell copy, neat'y triplicated, and lying unheeded with the single word, 'Perdition', in red as follows:

Fellows, remains, contrary-men, lend us your shears. We come to borrow scissors, not to prose. We the undersired, the undesired, the undesigned, the undeserving poor—poor we, powee, wish to express, wish to protest, wish to excise our right as humble bayings, wish to exercise our unaided, our inane, bare right arms, to cut it out, to cut it all off in its pretence, in its pride, to cut it all up (o this is unburdenable, unborn, impardonable, this too much measure of too much grievance, too cleavered in half), to curtail it short, slick it into little pieces, o into any kind of peace however sliced however slight, what severed scythe at all, a cloven square foot, to see all this long ailment come to a cut-ending, no other way to carve or cure it. To see the fin of all this ocean motion, the sudden shark that cuts through all the tidings, all this up and down, this double babble. We come to bury see-saws, not to play. Yours fatefully, two hopeless hacks, signed and resigned by Mr. Chinn and Mr. E.

With that, it seemed, he both had left his upper storey, his dislodging. Perhaps he had gone out still in his nursery garble (perhaps he no longer cowered), or perhaps he had simply rented all his clothes. In any case, in any cast-offs, he had gone clean out of his sentences and out into the world unasked, off into the wilderness with the sole aim of trying to collect to gather as many sick natures as humanely possible.

STRESS

'I am become,' he said, 'a drone, a useless thing, a monody, a monotone. And when I drum,' said he, 'upon my note, what people hear is all the same, the harping melody of all my plaint, the simple measure of my play, the humming of my pain. I am the hum ad nauseam, God knows I am, good news I damn. I chant my pain as plain as deal, a single note to every word, a single word to every dole. And if I had the power of speech, and if I had the power of song, my chants would be a finer thing. But when I sing, as sing I must, of harms to man, and means to ends, an end to all, and all to dust, some seem to stop and stare a while, and even some to know my song. It is to them I sing along, it is to them I long to bring the sullen solace of a song. So when I ask, O who, o who along the English coast will hear me?—I know the answer's in their glances, the only reason's in their straining. They know the argue of my speaking, they know the aching in my thought. I sing to them among the strong the endless versus of my song, my hymn and theme, my hush and utter. I share their moaning, I shape my meaning to their demeaning. I am the bard of all the barred, the true-bidder of all the bad, the minstrel of the mean. With me they go into the mountains, with me they play amongst the fountains, with me they lie about the meadows. For all the rest, I have no time, no tune, no muse, no news, and all they know of me is what they hear, and what there is to hear, in all and sum,' he said, 'is nothing but the endless whine of my iambic hum.'

PARADIGMS
LOST

He poured it out, without stinting, without understanding, all his old whinging into new imbecilities, new rebuttals. He had always tried ways of muting new people, of blunting them with his lack of silence, passing on to them his infantile lunacy, his little inchheights. And now he preached his thirst at any opening, any perished pump or public house or hall or where he might be stumped, on any strutting corner, any marked square. He was always speaking rough, always turning up and turfing out of towns or villas. He had in the outback of his outcast mind, in some hindered quarters, a half-balked idea of a gathering of the possessed and dispossessed, an army (ah me) of the saints and senseless, a crushed aid for the cursed, an unpleasants' reviling of the great unwished.

But no one would ever journey in his appalled grim agitation, his rally and trawling amongst the vicious of men, his mad marching of the hare-brained and heart-broken. He was left, laughed at, all a loon.

Except that he knew now for sudden that he was being followed. Not by his fallen-low fellow triflers, but without the poor least shadow of a dot followed in all the sleek-rat places, all the shared owings, by a legion of his long-time cravers to whom he owed his doubts, cur-editors and bookie-shopkeepers to whom his grumbling debts and dubious copy was overdue, lend-lords and pane-breakers to whom his ruin was owing, and rent-paying parents to whom the ruing of their sonny-gyms was in arrears. Purse-accused and sued by all his old animus, by everyone akin to him. O aye, he was being watched. Their corps of sprites, of spy-detectors into whose many-armed webbery they were trying to cash up with him, get him to court, were everywhere on the outlook for him, Mr. Chinn, pub-liking enigma number one. Slyly and surly, they were clustering in on him. His life of grime was coming to an end.

They trailed him, on a tip-off, to an open space, to a tip where his opinions were taking flight. They mangled themselves amongst the gathering crudes, cumulative and nimble, and watched for the chance to catechize him out, to ask him the unanswerable question, the ridicule of the thinks. He would go up to people, innocent by any standards, and try to tell them chokes, to make them laugh him, or to split their sides with his razor-sharp wittering. And if they were stern against him, or tried to get him stoned, he would rush to his own de-fence, sit on it (non com, admittedly), and probably make a break or fall over it, splintering the seemings in his pants.

When he had made his get-away, or so he fought, he would find himself a new campaign-site, a new battle pitch for the night, where he might find a moment's respiring smuggled

161

warmth in someone else's sleeping-bag, or a bread-roll snack in their shopping-bag. And when they chased him out of there, out of that traced pasture, he could only make good his escapade by cadging a double-defecting bus. He sat on the top, tired out of his mind (he needed arrest), taking his favourite back-seat, and still blowing his own last tramper's trumpet, trying to get a note out of it, a B-sharp with which he could keep himself alerted, not D-flatted, until it was time to alight.

But there was no final fare-escape, no getting away with or without it. It was way past the time for someone with his lost orders. They caught him up and out in the nick, two scot-free yeoman of the yard. They cuffed him about a bit with their hands, and read out the full terrific tarrif, the list of charges.

'You are under our wrist,' they said, 'and we should warrant you that everything you touch will be sawn off and may be used with irreverence against you. You are charged with attempting man's laughter. With behaviour likely to cause a piercing of the breeches, or to crush a fence. With loitering within tent. And with oompah-tuning in a public conveyance. Is there anything you wish to sigh?' He declined the officer. 'I must therefore ask you to come, ill foe, with us.'

TO COURT, AND A FUGUE (IN THE MORRIS MINOR)

After a night in salutary confinement, unshriven and addressed in ragtime, Mr. Chinn made a dishevelled appearance before a Major Straight, a cross ex-army noddy, a crusty justice of the hot pursuit. There was a mountainous mutinous pile of heresy evidence against him, of shock-'em substantial iffy-davits, upon which his reparation hung unbalanced, and to which a sick-session of sub-bound witnesses would give their testy moans. It was a small misery his parents could not be called to death-defy against him, cold as they were in their own witless boxes.

First to be pejorative was his old pedant all-agog Mr. Able, who said that the accusative was bound to lose the case, had never been willing to abide the rules, the laws and subordinating claws of the kings and keens of ink-land, had never

163

used a proper name, and always suffered from split affinities. He was followed into the misunderstanding by Mrs. Watser, who wept herself into a fine forensic frenzy as she remembered his sharp practices, how he had harplessly tried to copy her keys, how he had truly trillingly murdered Bacchus and Bovine and Beaux-Art with brutal fortissimos and uncontrollable violins.

Then claimed his Paris madame, his French père-confessor, his college tu-toi, that Mr. Chinn had barely been able to tell his masculine from his feminine endings, which Val and Simeon, his first belle-ovid best beloveds, next in the box, both blared out. And after them, the army-guerdoned magical officer who had grounded him for his lungs' listless heaving, or peaceably the one who had granted him his long last leavetaking, under the rules of the pox britannica, and who now took his hypocritical oath that Mr. Chinn had the jaw of a gaol and the face of a safe-breaker, and the all-round cranium of a criminal type.

Then there was the head of his finishing school, the school that had finished him, who bore now a false whiteness, a hair-aid on his bald-faced headpiece, to the effect of all Mr. Chinn's many missed team-meetings, demeaning his teaching, and telling tales out of school about his failures with the fifth, his crushes and defeats and other defections. The antic dealer who had bought off him his three puny bits, swore on the buyable, swore bland, swore black and ballooned like a salesman, that he had been chatted, diluted, bum-boozed, his expenses defrauded, his ale-money whittled down, and that the diffident was no better than a cowman thief, a poacher whom he reproached with preying on the insolent.

And then it was Maud who brazenly breezily regaled the whole tense court with her backhanded underhanded game, the old racket, the same old balls, a packet of lies and under-lies and half-sleuths, the trash, the old trash, and nothing bitterer than the trash. And Keith too, keen Keith, the captain of his fatal stocky hockey team, even he, the eleventh man at the eleventh hour, was willing to take his stand and say that all their funny business and gaming was not what it had seemed, was unseemly what it dissembled not to be, and gave the claim away on all Mr. Chinn's good pretensions.

Last in the dock, the doctor and the nurse, the first to say that he was well and truly marred, a shit-soiled personality, living in a spilt poison reality, and that his only chink of escape was to plead insanitary, to claim that he was not in the fooled possession of his fickle-ties, his former clanliness, his mend-all fuck-all tidinesses. And the soft-spoken second to tell how he had dragooned and drugged her, clobbered and dragged off her all her clobber in an act of daylight delighted disrobery, a travesty of injustice.

These were the faker's dozen good-for-nothing men and trulls who spiked against him. Where was there someone anywhere who could sparkle in his defiance? It was Bruce who came, blathering late and nerveless, and who warbled in his fervour, saying how much his friend was worth, how high in his extreme, what a janus, what a herod, what a shy-ant amongst men. As always he made it all uproarious as he went along, garbling unaided meanings out of the thin air, and never waiting for applause. Bruce had always been a newer sense in Mr. Chinn's long knowing, but now he was a paean in the nick.

They asked him how he bleeded, guillotinely or not cleanly. They asked him if he had anything to save for himself. All along he had been subdued, d'you see, but now he wanted to say that this, in a sense, was his whole deaf-ending, the unheard-of vices all squawking beside him, the hole in his heed when he tried to speak, not knowing how to put what spoke in, what was allowed, and what in a lisper, to what slammed chance of a slander he was liable—and yet still wanton to speak, to say his beholden piece. But he

165

un-sweared nothing to the pleads, only to ask for many other lacks of conviction to be taken into account. And then, in a sobbing last outbreak, something that was overdue inside him, the knowledge that he had always been a loaner and a freeman with his boroughings, the half-reminder of how late and huge and fine it had all been, made him raise to his feet and hurl and cry at the whole sitting bunch of them, 'I'll return my books!'

The grandfather clerk tried to re-train him, ticked him off. His own lawyer, no-one embarrasseder, asked for his supplicant to be led off politely—he wanted to see him hugged, drawn out, and acquitted. The Major's valediction was that he should be reminded of his cursed-daddy, his bastardy, and remaindered in Hatchard's for some further futile days. But before anything also could be said or done, Mr. Chinn had slipped out of their gasps, charged into the straight outside and into a car, an old gaol-hopper just like his Dad's, and had driven off feeling as the wind, blowing his honour at all the ass-townish inhibitors who saw his latest greatest caper.

GOODBYE
MR. CHINN

H ad he still not given himself up, even after so much trial and terror, was he still wanting to get somewhere in his own way after all, as he spurred down the martyr-way, exhilarating on every blind bender as he went? Where was he going in his own mind, driving himself to the very edge it seemed, to the seamy side, coasting along without encountering the cosseting he had always needed, returning himself you might have construed it to the very waters the very same simple-pool from which he sprang, shutting himself in with the same quayside, or setting himself at risk on the whirled open wastes, the streaming gulfs, of the uncharitable the uncherubic carib-aeon neverending sea, down into the last scylla-pool of regardless time—was that where he was deemed?

Before he came to his junket's end, to the junk-yard of old crack-ups and escaped scrapped metal-cases where he would ultimately pitch his carcass, he thought he'd stop first to scale his unassailable thirst, a cup all-round of drinks ('And one for years' health, sir,' he said to the beer-man), a swigger or two before turning himself in. He knew, do you see, clearly what was taking his place, the crime-axe that was approaching, the two-horsepower engine at the door. The die was cast, the rest of the cast was as good as dead. The rest of the strategy, the tragedy, was unfolding up even as he intensified it. Now he was lonely having a drink in the end-of-all, a last half before the finality, before the groaned fie-nihility, one for the riddance, for the folded-roles that had played themselves out.

His last stop of all was at the unfeeling patrol-station, where he fuelled her up, and two guileful cans to be on the safe side, no point in running out at this stretch of the game. The plump and tender pump-attendant looked at him queerly as he gave him his last chance for a change, blinked at him and smiled blankly. Have I got a smut on my nose, thought Mr. Chinn, or is he so smart he thinks he knows, sees through my canny planning, can he? He pushed back through the open window a little tipsy, a bunch of fivers, more usury to you than where I'm going, he said, and putting his foot down, wouldn't take no for an answer, sped his way out of the garish lights and onto the darkening beckoning open road.

Now he was there, his dark futures, his night-maze, mabbed out scarcely before him, clear on the foreshore, the wondering all stilled to a hard-beating in his head, the wind in his hair, the impeding storm still brooding in the air, the guttering clouds. He looked back along the ghost to where the lights were twinkling in his eye—that way widnes lies, he thought, or lever-pull or man's great jester, I am well away from there. He was in distant sight of the caravans beyond him and the pale tints at all points of the campers around. No one to know 'tis him, no one near enough to curb or care, no wonder. He was as soft, as delicate, as tinder as touch, ready to go off at any, if there had been any body there, and not just him bare in his mind, him and the beach, the cold heartless beach (o fore-grieve me), the mind-numberless sands, and behind him the wind-irked sea.

He knew all the ways of making an ending, had reversed them over to himself on many resented occasions in the past. There was nothing he deadened know about draining your life away with a long cresting stroke far out into abandoned living, into oblivion, the water way to go. Or about the long jump, the high jump from a headlong cleft-top, from sheer cliff-hankerings, or the throwaway line into an on and oncoming train or trailer. He knew about everything to do with lethal bits of pills or poison-pains or pipes fixed to the point of exhaustion or sticking your head in the auvergne or suffolk-hating or anything to do with plugging up your courage and twitching on at the mains, the mania, the many failed-proven ways of giving up the jest, the cost of living. He knew all the latest nooses, the knots to know to hang it all from under a tree, sub judas, and he knew too the crazy fiction that this would raise an erection in a hangman, the happy ending, the final fling. He had taught himself about the slow easy oozing of his life-blush by taking his final wrists or his idle throat slipped through in a puke-warm bath. He had even had odd thoughts of gutting himself down, harum-scarum sharp'n'easy style, of setting out and about to catch himself a deathly pox, a fever in his crap, or fasting himself to a slow death, a faim fatale, or bewraying himself, sod upon clot upon clod, in his own early gravy, his own glowery hole. He was a veritable variable walking do-in-yourself manual, a begoners' guide.

But here on the infirm stranding, on the shift and drift half-away between the sea and the land, in the bitch bleakness of the night, and with all of a time-past coming to a head to a dead ending, he had chosen (chosen! what a word for that void, for what there was no knowing of, nothing there, in his emptied amputated brain-tub), he had found himself fanned himself into alighting himself (stoke the world, he wanted to get off lightly), into setting himself up as a star (a drink-all drunken little star), whose flame would spread across all inland, an arch-beacon, a saving plight-house making out the point of greatest dinge, the darkest deepness. He had always yearned, burned since birth to emulate himself, and now he would be making himself a beautiful pyre, the true two of himself he had always been. Maybe he would be playing the fuel, playing with matches in this way, but he would also be praying for a true fire-nullity, for the cease which passes undeserving, the blazing of the father and the son and the whole spirit, the risky-doubles he had tanked inside him, and the poor patrimony the stormy petrol the opprobrium he poured and poured on onto his poor self, anointing himself now in the nought-time, now in the markless, now in the end.

He took his shoes off on the sand, put them paired to one side. Shunned only his shoes, and kept on his tread-bare coat, his oldest hick's jacket until the bitter rend. He was not going to make his quitting, his quiet exit, with his boddikins all bare. He would go in clothing as he had been born in the opening, distressed for the equation.

And then began his little dance, as the first sparks caught, and the storming in the havens picked up its rancour. His tiddled answer to the first beginnings of the reddish flame fire. He made his first valse-step with little hastening, little hesitation, and then another with hardly a pause. And soon he was thingumajigging and bobbing on the shore, a tango of flame waving on the beach, his so-alone god-stepping pas de dieu, singeing and dancing in the rain. Hopping mad.

And the waters came, came gushing down his face and

crashing in waves behind his feet. And the storming came on and on, in the sea-cloud sick loud too much tumult of it all. And did all of his life pass before him in an enlightening flash before he died, from that first dunderheaded wonder-clap to this? And did he know all-over to home-again, the whole sorry story, as he went up in mockery, went up in smoke, burning to a sundering? And what did it matter, and what was he muttering, as the first of the hail-day folk saw what was happening, as it dawned on them what was that fabled feeble fire-ball on the beach, the tongue all of flame and falling over itself and flailing in the first glimmers? And what had he maybe been saying against the wind and the wavings and the over-welkin, against them all, as the first of the van-guards came down to the sands and poked a finger at the dismal embers? And the waters came, came dashing in where the ash was strewn, came lashing, and cleansed him tidally away.

BITCHERY

We are sorry to denounce the death of Mr. Chinn, from a curse as yet unknown, the building up of bile and the raising of bail to boiling-point over many years, from which the burst was always yet to come. His life was one of unending surface and te deum. The treachery of his eerie dismissal will be filtered by all. He will be sordidly messed by his friends and remembered as an extinguished figment in many fields, a free man (hardly) and will-less, and as a persona (none greater).

Mr. Chinn was whelped into this world by model-class arents who gave him all their spare parts. He was eradicated at the nation's most inspected pubescent skills, where his eager-demented achievements were considerable, and where he sported rose to grey tights in cross-border gin-running, for which he was kept in.

After hired education and an early mortgage, from which he came away with the expected decree, the usual scullery-duggery, he served with distraction amongst His Magnificently Formed Arses, where his come-on touch was wildly appreciated amongst his feral-officers as much as by the other wanks.

He had the ability to be all things, the desire to do all awful things to all men and women. He could doubtfully have been an extremely immanent philosopher, a righter, a punter, a classy magician, a don with his voluminous notes, a queer's consoler, a mumbler of paramount, a star of the sylvan serene. Instead, after minatory service, he chose to return his affection to the need for boys and became a devoured and revealed school-martyr, where many members of generations will still recoil from him heartily. In the spittoon-bars and communion-rooms that he freely quitted, he was fondlingly known to all as a git, born vagrant, and wreck in tears.

Mr. Chinn, he-lass, is dead, and a loss, no longer witters. He leaves behind him an estranged feint whiff, and two chilblains, a sinister and a brooder, from an earlier mirage. He will be remembered with a fiction.